DEATH REEL

Death Reel

HAMISH MacINNES

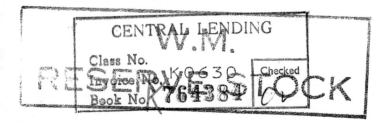

HODDER AND STOUGHTON
LONDON SYDNEY AUCKLAND TORONTO

To the doctors and staff,
Ward 10, Edinburgh Royal Infirmary

2186

*Copyright ©1976 by Hamish MacInnes. First printed 1976.ISBN 0 340 20725
6. All rights reserved. No part of this publication may be reproduced or
transmitted in any form or by any means, electronic or mechanical,
including photocopy, recording, or any information storage and retrieval
system, without permission in writing from the publisher. Phototypesetting
by Saildean Ltd. Printed in Great Britain for Hodder and Stoughton
Limited, London by Billing & Sons Ltd., Guildford, London and Worcester.*

1

THE BLACK GEMINI was rowed skilfully, but its progress was slow as it rounded the rocky headland. Over his left shoulder the oarsman could pick out the white pebble-dash walls of the Point House and he eased the boat closer to the shore, where there was cover from rhododendrons on the margin of the cliff.

He dropped a small anchor. With a professional tug to make sure it held, he tied the line off to the bows. Then he put on an aqualung over his dry suit and turned on the high-pressure cylinder. It read 4,000 psi on the luminous dial. Putting his head between the twin pipes he gripped the mouthpiece between strong, even teeth. He wore no goggles. With an easy movement, he spilled over into the dark water.

In the night shadows on the lawn of the Point House a large man in dark trousers and pullover ran soundlessly down the concrete steps to a boathouse built into the cliff face.

From the water level the visitor's discreet torch probed the interior of the boathouse. It picked out a cutter. There was a sudden eruption behind him: the flash of a blade and a simultaneous rush of escaping air. The light sank slowly a few feet away from the cutter, and two figures surfaced, threshing wildly, now in the deeper water outside. The engine of an inflatable coughed, then roared into life and a wide beam of light reached out across the water. The boathouse was framed open-mouthed. The motor slammed viciously into gear and the boat shot towards the combatants as they went under again.

The visitor kicked himself free of the human ballast and surfaced beside the boat. He reached up and grabbed at its occupant. Then hands gripped him from below and he felt himself drawn irresistibly downwards. The boat moved forward, a forcible blow from above broke his hold on the clothing, and he spun round and down, one outflung arm catching the screw of the outboard. His struggling became feebler...

2

Cliff Dempster opened a glass door. He had been walking this floor with long even strides for five minutes, through a forest of absorbed typists. The atmosphere seemed a cross between the sanctity of a monastery and the ruthless efficiency of an assembly line.

The door closed behind him automatically. Some very effective sound-proofing had been deployed, whilst a Chinese carpet gobbled up any stray decibels. Not that the typing pool had been noisy; rather the subdued hum of a contented hive. Some nice prints adorned the white walls, but he didn't know enough about art to put a price tag on them. An Andrea Brustelon armchair stood in one corner. In the middle of the room, behind a large walnut desk, sat Swartze's secretary. She appeared, Dempster noted approvingly, as shapely and as well designed as the rest of the expensive office furnishings.

"Mr Dempster?" Her smile was friendly, her eyes green and set wide apart. She looked Nordic, he thought, with that very blond hair and clear skin.

"Yes, I've an appointment at two-thirty." His accent was hybrid. "To see Mr Swartze."

"Won't you take a seat?"

"I'd rather stand."

"Please do sit down. Mr Swartze may be a few minutes. You'll make me nervous, watching me from such a height." She gave him another smile, but there was no response. He looked in his late thirties, she decided, his skin burnt brown with years of exposure to the sun. A life on the open sea, she guessed, wrongly. His two-piece white suit was new and his white shirt open at the neck. Casual, very casual, but not untidy. He seemed too sure of himself to look untidy.

After a few seconds he went over to the only other chair available, placed to catch the maximum light from the large plate-glass window which served as one wall and allowed an uninterrupted view over the City. Turning his gaze from a panorama which evidently appeared distasteful to him, he noted, above the head of the blond Aglaiope and slightly higher than the top edge of the Persian carpet, several ornamental recesses, each about a hand span square, set with delicately tinted glass in lead mouldings. The centre one had clear glass with lead moulding only round the edges. The chandelier which hung above the desk appeared to have a very low light output to that particular section of wall. Dempster looked directly at the aperture, gave a hard cynical smile, and raised his right forefinger to his brow in a derisive salutation.

The girl had returned her gaze to a paper on her desk. Dempster was to be given up to one hour with Mr Swartze — AND, meaning in Swartze language 'And No Disturbance'. Normally only cabinet ministers and international oil moguls could command such inroads into her boss's most valuable commodity. A light glowed on her desk.

"Mr Swartze will see you now, Mr Dempster." She stood up, smiled dutifully, and crossed towards a polished walnut door. Her legs were long, bare and brown. Dempster realised that she was taller than he had first imagined, and she moved with a supple grace. He surprised himself with a fleeting mental picture of her cross-country skiing.

"Mr Dempster," she announced briefly.

The President of Consolidated Oil looked up at Dempster over a bare desk and an expanse of purpleheart flooring. Obviously a tycoon who scorned to underline the image with ostentatious papers and a battery of telephones. His fat, round bespectacled face was belied by a sharp ski-jump nose. Perched toadlike on

8

the edge of his swivel chair, glasses flashing, he appeared disarmingly to be trying to muster enough confidence to leap across the expanse of austere luxury between himself and his visitor. But Dempster knew that here was a man every bit as decisive as himself. Probably more ruthless. Beady eyes bored through him like high-speed drills.

"Thank you, Tania." The voice which dismissed her was precise, with the meticulous diction of a foreigner who has mastered the language. Swartze did not get up, or offer to shake hands. He merely waved Dempster to a chair. He didn't offer cigarettes either, as he knew his visitor didn't smoke. He knew a lot about Dempster; he had studied his dossier carefully, some of the details of which would have amazed the tall dark man in the white suit who sat impassively waiting for the interview to begin. Swartze didn't like or dislike people. If they were efficient, they were acceptable; if not, he didn't bother with them.

Dempster was acceptable, he knew that.

Efficient and ruthless. Clifford Dempster, he recalled, aged thirty-seven. He looked older. A Scot by birth. Yes, he could see that, the austere look with a touch of Celtic blood, or Fian, perhaps. Resident of California. Hitherto, Dempster had operated for Consolidated Oil from the States, but a climbing vacation in the French Alps had made him conveniently accessible in a hurry.

It was only two days earlier that he had received a personal telephone call from Swartze at the Hotel des Alpes, Chamonix, requesting him to fly over to London immediately. Dempster had known better than to ask questions over the phone and his curiosity was more than a little roused by the involvement of the top man at Consolidated Oil.

Now, brushing aside conversational preliminaries, Swartze favoured him with a smile. "Allow me, firstly, to congratulate you. You are the only person to have detected my closed-circuit TV. I like to preview my visitors. Though in your case I think it would have been a wasted exercise. I doubt if you ever advertise your emotions, Mr Dempster."

Dempster offered no comment, his face suitably impassive as he waited.

"I have been very satisfied with what you have done for our company in the States," Swartze continued. "I am only sorry we have not met before. But perhaps it is just as well," he indulged in another smile, "since it would have meant I had found some trouble requiring your attention. I was most impressed, incidentally, by your handling of that Nepal assignment," he added smoothly.

Dempster's eyelid flickered for an instant as his mental computer raced to work out how the devil this leptodactylus had learnt about the job in Chinese Tibet. Only one other person had known of his involvement in that operation and it shook him to discover it had found its way onto a file, however confidential. What else did Swartze know? He obviously had an expensive crystal ball.

"You are a Scot, Mr Dempster." Swartze had changed tack. But at least it was a proposition to which his visitor could give assent.

"The land of oil and plenty," he returned equably, wondering if this would be sufficient to lead the smaller man safely back to the point of his visit.

"Exactly so. Exactly so." Swartze beamed like a fisherman whose bait has been accepted at the first cast. "And I want you to go back there for me. We are working off the west coast at present. An area of considerable potential. Let me show you." Swartze produced a map and spread it on the top of his desk. Dempster went over to him. "Consolidated Oil have plans for a very large refinery in north-west Scotland, Mr Dempster. It will be the biggest in Europe." He pinned one side of the map with his forearm, while Dempster obligingly held the other. "Here's the Thule field, to the north and west. There's deep water here." He stabbed the blue area to the west of the coastline with his forefinger. "And we can take a submarine pipeline in from the platforms. This is the territory we need." He ran a finger round a purple outline which included a stretch of rugged coast. Dempster examined it closely. "It's the march of the Rhuda estate," Swartze explained.

"Rhuda?"

"Yes. We want it. Do you know the area at all?"

10

"Let me see," the large man mused, gazing at the map. "Yes, of course. Inverloch, Beinn Dearg. I've climbed there. Who owns the estate?"

Swartze's mouth tightened. "A cantankerous old devil called Hector McBride."

"Who won't sell?"

"I thought he was going to assault me when I went to see him personally. He refuses point blank to deal with us."

"But I thought there was government legislation now to deal with such — local difficulties?"

"There is, but Rhuda is not a scheduled development area, so compulsory purchase could take time. And time is one commodity we can't afford in this business."

"And what am I supposed to do for you, Mr Swartze? I hardly think my Scots blood is going to be sufficient to endear me to your laird."

"Ah, no. It's another man altogether I want you to keep an eye on for me." Swartze allowed the map of north-west Scotland to roll itself up again. The geography lesson was over. He sat back in his swivel chair, fingers braced on the desk before him and chose his words carefully.

"One of our geologists called Wilson, Paul Wilson. He's a first-class man, but he needs watching. You know about the off-shore oil business from your activities in Venezuela, so I need hardly tell you that a geologist connected with test drilling holds a very responsible position and we have given Paul Wilson a free hand. He has always worked better that way. No, the matter that worries me is a letter." Swartze gave an almost apologetic cough before continuing, and examined the neat half-moons of his nails. "Recently, on the advice of the Ministry of Defence, we began taking a more stringent look at our internal security. Installed scrambler Telexes, that sort of thing. And about a month ago I introduced spot checks on outgoing mail, from the rigs, survey ships, offices and so on..."

"And?"

"And, Mr Dempster, I found Paul Wilson had written a very curious letter to a young man called James McBride, son of the stone-walling laird."

11

"Curious, in what way?"

"Young McBride has been seen with Wilson. It appears they went to college together, so the fact they've met up again doesn't mean much on the face of it. Wilson is working in the Little Minch area at present, on our survey vessel, the *Celtic Pioneer*. Inverloch is their operational base. It's where, incidentally, we are opening a new co-ordination centre in the very near future."

"And the letter?" Dempster prompted.

Swartze reached once more into his desk and drew out a thin manilla folder. There weren't many papers in it. The top one was a photostat, which he passed over to his visitor with evident distaste. Dempster saw it was a copy of a letter, dated merely "Kyle, Tuesday".

Dear James,

I hope that you have chewed over our friend's proposals properly by this time and come to the right conclusions. Believe me, it's the sort of scheme that could do us both a lot of good. But you've got to get a move on. For a start, I hope you are piling the pressure on your old man to sell out. Time is rolling on and you will have to get your finger out. The last thing we want is to give Consolidated Oil time to apply legal screws. We must get in first. So let's meet once you've softened up father, and before you do another of your famous disappearing acts, James. I seem to remember you had a convenient talent for that sort of thing not so very long ago.

Did I tell you that I met Fazil in Karachi, by the way? He talked a lot about you.

Get to work on the old man again James, and I'll see you when I'm next in Inverloch.

Yours,
Paul

"It sounds as though you may not be the only party interested in the Rhuda estate," observed Dempster dryly.

"Of course, of course." Swartze brushed aside the obvious. "It's a prime site for any oil company. But I don't like my employees getting involved with third parties, Dempster. Especially men as important as Paul Wilson."

"Have you faced him with this?" Dempster put down the photostat.

"No. The original letter was delivered to McBride." Swartze made a slight grimace. "What I want you to do is cover Wilson. Here's his dossier." He slid the slim folder across his desk to Cliff Dempster. "Nothing unusual there. Take it away if you wish. He's been working for us for nine years. It's all there. I want you to find out exactly what is going on between Wilson and this young McBride. Now he's a bit of an odd character by all accounts. Nobody knows much about him. He *has* been living abroad. But if anybody's going to buy the Rhuda estate, it's going to be me."

"How large is it? Rhuda?"

"Eighteen thousand acres."

"Quite a hunk of land!"

"A wilderness. I don't know how anyone could hold even the remotest affection for it," Swartze replied tetchily.

"What exactly do you want me to do, Mr Swartze?"

"You're a free agent, naturally, but I suggest that you make your way to Inverloch. The *Celtic Pioneer* berths there when not involved in survey. You will be visiting as an observer from an old established British oil company, UK Lubricants. And it's been given out generally that you're a nephew of old Sir Hubert Lamphrey, the Managing Director, who's been threatening to retire for the past five years. It's been hinted also that you may be asked to join the board and that you want to acquire a first hand knowledge of all aspects of the business. As we work closely with Sir Hubert, it's quite natural that you should be offered our facilities, and we do have observers from time to time." Pride in running a show piece of the oil world showed momentarily in the small man's voice. But he returned quickly to his briefing. "Your name is Hugh Spencer, born in Edinburgh. You know it?"

"Enough."

"The real Spencer, Lamphrey's nephew, is living in Tahiti at present, so it's a convenient cover. Not one hundred per cent but good enough for a short period. You'll find the details in the file."

"Sir Hubert Lamphrey has agreed to play ball?"

"Oh yes. As a matter of fact he was in the army with old McBride, the 3rd Royal Horse Artillery, I think. So I can ask him to write to McBride, if you like, to say you might just make a courtesy call while you're in the district. Give you a chance to see the lie of the land."

"That sounds a good idea. Tell me, couldn't Sir Hubert have helped with the purchase of the property?"

"I thought of that. Hubert did sound out the old boy, without actually asking directly, but it was no use. It was after that that I went to see the man myself." Swartze drew a discreet veil over defeat and returned to the subject in hand. "One thing more. It is customary for us to provide our visitors with a guide and I have asked Tania Olsen, my secretary, whom you have met outside, to fulfill this role, as I have to be in the States for the next week or so." Cliff Dempster opened his mouth to speak and closed it again, as the oil man continued. "I can delegate considerable powers to Miss Olsen, which may help you. Also Captain Craig, the master of the *Celtic Pioneer*, has been told to offer you all facilities, and one of our best pilots will have his helicopter at the co-ordination centre in case you require it. I will hope, Mr Dempster," Swartze concluded briskly, "that you have some reassurance to give me when I come to Scotland at the end of the month for the official opening of our new centre."

"You seemed pretty certain of me." Dempster smiled wryly and rose to his feet. "And you've covered most things. What, however, if there's nothing to find out?"

"If you discover nothing, you will at least have set my mind at rest. I dislike being bothered by untidy details. It takes my mind off more important business. But I don't want our employees to think they are being spied upon. It's bad for efficiency and it's bad for morale and, normally, it's against my principles. Two thousand pounds has been deposited, as an advance, under your name with the Midland Bank, Leicester Square..."

"When do you want me to start?" He felt an unwilling flicker of kinship with this dynamic Billy Bunter. A Bunter with an appetite for wheeler dealing, who disliked unexplained fragments of information floating around. Dempster had the same sort of tidy brain himself.

"There's just one thing," he said, gazing down with studied care at the blank cover of the manilla folder in his strong broad hands.

"That is?"

"I don't know if I fancy a woman in the scenario. I suppose she could distract attention from me. Particularly your Miss Olsen, I should imagine. But at the same time she's bound to hamper my movements."

Swartze's expression did not brook argument. "I don't think you will find Tania hampering you, she's an extremely resourceful girl, very competent. And remember she could give you a sound psychological advantage. Anyone sent to spy on my employees, Mr Dempster, would be expected to do it more — surreptitiously."

Swartze smiled the smile of a Buddha sharing an unspoken joke with a divine presence. The interview was evidently over.

3

Cliff Dempster had left Scotland when he was twenty. Sitting beside Tania in the Consolidated Oil Mercedes, nosing smoothly through the first of the rush-hour traffic next morning, he suddenly realised how much he was looking forward to getting back there. He could still see the Cuillin on a clear spring evening with the Minch lit by that fairy glow, a footlight for the raised islands, the crescent of the gabbro ridge.

Yes, it would be good to see Scotland again. Perhaps he would even get in some climbing. Studying Paul Wilson's file after his meeting with Swartze, he had discovered the geologist was a keen mountaineer. Not quite in his own class, of course. Cliff had been on several Himalayan expeditions. Hugh Spencer of UK Lubricants wouldn't be in that class either, he reminded himself. But he could safely pretend to some weekend climbing ability.

Remembering Wilson's file, Cliff brooded on how many dossiers such as this were stowed away in safes and filing cabinets throughout London. Big brothers watching, recording, watching...obituaries written long before celebrities kicked their respective buckets. Here he was in the vile jungle of big business, harvesting information and preparing to swell the personal file of some probably entirely innocent individual. A kindred thought naggingly reasserted itself. Where the hell had that fat turd dug up the information on the Nepalese job? Only four people had known about that sortie into Tibet and only one knew that he personally was involved. Yet Swartze had somehow managed to exhume this interesting titbit...

"He's an impressive man, your Mr Swartze." He addressed Tania for the first time since the perfunctory civilities of meeting and setting out for the airport.

"He is indeed." She was surprised. She had expected disapproval, and now made a renewed effort at conversation. "Is this your first visit to Scotland, Mr — er — Spencer?" She put the name in careful inverted commas.

"Cliff," he offered abruptly, "for the time being that is. I was born there." His voice carried no hint of warmth or desire to prolong the conversation. It was obvious no further personal information would be forthcoming.

Swartze, who believed in equipping his staff with all the relevant facts for the job, had told Tania of Dempster's lack of enthusiasm for her company. He had also, briefly, explained the real purpose of his visit, and her part in the cover he would be using. Tania had taken guests round Consolidated's Scottish enterprises three times before and always enjoyed her visits to the north-west, meeting welcoming people and having a pleasant holiday in the fresh air, away from the hectic life of the main office. She hoped this tall, sunburnt man with his curt manners and his devious mission wasn't going to spoil everything. Looking sideways at him, under the guise of watching for the approach to the airport feed road, she could get no impression of what went on behind those dark guarded eyes. His large frame appeared relaxed, but at the same time gave the impression of a tremendous pent-up force, ready at an instant to be released. Her eyes dropped to his hands and she noticed for the first time that the little finger was missing on Dempster's left hand. She wondered idly how he had lost it.

"Frostbite."

She coloured momentarily. "You seem to be able to read my mind." Privately she thought it was a misfortune entirely in keeping with his manners. But at that moment the big car which had been threading its way between airport buildings drew to a halt near a trim private Trilander. They had arrived.

As Tania led the way across the tarmac, Cliff had grudgingly

17

to admit that she was one of the few women he had seen in trousers who didn't look as if her centre of gravity had moved down eighteen inches since she last wore a skirt.

"Meet Jack Bourne, Mr Spencer." Tania was making the introductions. "He's one of our pilots from the fleshpots of Canada. A Home Rule for Quebec man, if the truth be known."

"Hiya, Spencer." Bourne was a thickset man with bushy eyebrows and a cap set back at a jaunty angle. "I'm taking you to Dyce. If you're ready, Tania, hop aboard and let's go."

As he saw to the baggage and closed the hatch behind Dempster, the Canadian pilot looked at his passenger more closely.

"Haven't I seen you some place before, Mr Spencer?"

"No, I don't think so. Though it's a small world these days." Cliff remembered the Canadian all right. He'd been a pilot with a firm he'd done a job for several years ago in Alaska. But they had never spoken or been introduced by name.

"Yes, I guess you're right. And it's our business that's made it that way. You in oil too?"

"A virtual newcomer, having a look round at present."

"Well there's sure plenty to see up there. You heading further north, or working from Aberdeen?"

"We're visiting the north west for a start," Tania explained. "Just a general look at everything, isn't that the idea, Mr Spencer?"

"That's right. I want to see just what makes the whole thing tick, from the drill bit to the petrol pump. Miss Olsen here is going to show me the ropes."

"Well, I guess she can show me her ropes any day," Jack Bourne replied with a grin.

The Trilander touched down at Aberdeen Dyce with the minimum of fuss. Dempster's last visit here, seventeen years before, had been to a one-horse airstrip with a few run-down shacks. Now hulking great Sikorsky helicopters crouched with drooping rotors like praying mantises. At the edge of the airfield a flock of small, brightly coloured planes clustered round the hangars. The sky was clear. Underfoot black tarmac gleamed with the wet sheen of fresh enamel. Jack Bourne had their luggage sent over to a modest blue Mini which would be theirs for the duration of their visit. Minis didn't seem quite Swartze's style, Cliff thought, until he noticed it was a special coachwork job with alloy wheels and eight inch wide racing tyres.

"This car's a bit of a wolf in sheep's clothing." Tania produced the keys. "At least, the way Mr Swartze drives it, it is. Something about a stage three engine which is his particular pride and joy." She laughed ruefully as she unlocked the driver's door and glanced at Cliff. "All I know is that it's a swine to drive at slow speeds and that it resembles a Mini only in looks."

"Must have a look at the mainspring sometime." Dempster showed a flicker of interest. "I appreciate good cars."

Obviously more than he does me, Tania thought a shade sourly, as she offered politely, "Do you want to drive?"

"Could do," he replied, coming round to her side of the car. "Get used to driving on the left again."

As he drove slowly out of the built-up area, he mentally regurgitated the file he had read on Wilson: thirty years old; five foot eleven; hair brown; Cambridge honours graduate in chemical engineering; employee of Consolidated Oil for the nine years since he left college. Did good work for the company in Alaska and the Sudan. One-time member of Cambridge University Mountaineering Club; took part in an exploration into Ladakh with five university friends, financed by various trusts. Scars on left leg from car accident in Iran when company Land-Rover was involved in a landslide; broke right leg while on vacation in the Yosemite Valley, California. Unpopular at college and with fellow employees at Consolidated Oil. Occasional girl friends, none steady. There were various photographs, mainly company shots and some taken at cocktail parties. Several newspaper cuttings and press reports of oil rigs and oil exploration work in which he had featured. There was also a column from the *San Francisco Star* two years earlier, about his accident in Yosemite. It had happened on a peak called El Capitan during a climb known as Aquarian. This struck a chord in Dempster's memory. He had been in Los Angeles at the time and vaguely remembered reading the local account.

Well, he'd manage to find something to talk to the man about, he supposed.

"You just follow the Inverness signposts now," Tania broke into his train of thought.

"Good," he grunted. "If I remember correctly, it's more or less straight through now."

At that precise moment, Jack Bourne walked into a call box within the terminal building at Dyce and dialled a number in Inverloch. For almost two minutes he spoke in rapid French.

On the long straights of the A96 through to Forres and Inverness, Cliff let the car run up to 120 mph and observed with pleasure that there was still plenty of kick there. The noise level was incredibly low. Noise suppression was one of Swartze's foibles, he decided.

"It's not that I'm nervous," there was a definite edge in Tania's voice, "nor am I a backseat driver, but there is a statutory speed limit on all British roads, in case you didn't know."

"Yes, of course. I tend to forget when I use the rev metre instead of the speedometer."

Cliff sounded almost cheerful. He had taken a look at the engine when they had topped up with petrol a few miles back, and laughed at the garage attendant.

"Hey, meester, that's some motor. A double knocker Lotus in a Mini! There's no' many like this aboot."

The engine was indeed a twin-cam Lotus 2-litre with four double-choke carburettors. Power, he noted, was trans-mitted through a five-speed ZF box, and to the front wheels via a transfer box. As Cliff closed the bonnet with a subdued click, he came to the conclusion that he approved of Swartze's toys.

After seventeen years of travelling about the world it came as a surprise to him to see the road improvements in northern Scotland. Tortuous corners and hills alike had been eliminated. He was getting the feel of the car now, after an introduction on the straights and one brief struggle with the seat — to push it far enough back for his long legs.

20

"This is a most beautiful desolate country," Tania remarked aloud. They were on that high section of road beyond Garve where it starts to dip gently to the head of the Coire Shellach gorge and the head of Loch Broom. "It reminds me of home." She was more or less talking to herself, not expecting an answer. When Cliff replied, it was something of a shock.

"Great place," he breathed appreciatively, as he slackened speed behind a lorry returning north with empty fish boxes. "But I think it'll be ruined by tourism and oil development."

She glanced sideways to see if he was feeling tired after his long speech. "Didn't some poet talk about killing the thing he loved?"

"Wilde — 'Reading Gaol'," Cliff returned absently.

They reached the tourist jampot of Ullapool too late for lunch and nosed cautiously through the congestion of five-generation-removed Americans back to pay homage to the clearances. At the Easy Eats counter of an establishment whose lack of patronage should have been its own warning, Cliff and Tania made do with coffee and ham sandwiches. The regulation 3 cc of brown sauce almost succeeded in making the latter look as tartan as everything else on display in that northern turning point of the Highland touring beat. Tania left half her coffee.

"Let's get going," Cliff said. "I'm sorry. We should have found somewhere sooner. These places are the same the world over. We have more than our fair share in LA, but the sandwiches are better there."

Outside, on the corner, a hoarse old man was trying to persuade the reluctant public to buy his few remaining newspapers. He sounded in need of a drink to restore his overworked vocal chords, and his loyalties were clearly divided between the undiminishing fistful of papers and the Prince Charlie bar opposite. A billboard behind him proclaimed the existence of the *West Highland Gazette and Advertiser*. Scribbled below in lurid purple ink was the highlight of the week's news: 'Lobster man dies at sea'.

"You want to drive now?"

"Had enough of the toy?"

"I'd like to follow the scenery. Much easier as a passenger!"

Tania drove fast and competently. Cliff smiled to himself at her earlier comments about the speed limit. Ahead of them a long low car moved out of a layby as she swept past with a blast of the horn.

"What kind of a car was that?"

"A Ferrari Boxer. Strange sight in these parts."

"It's a strange-looking machine altogether," she commented, keeping her eyes keenly on the road where a fast right hand bend was approaching. The Mini wasn't exactly crawling; in fact it was doing well over the ton, but there was a roar behind and a yellow blur as the Ferrari shot past, the twelve intakes of its Weber carburettors in two rows like sherry glasses behind the rear window.

"That's incredible," Tania gasped. "What a car!" She glanced at her speedometer. "He must be doing about 150."

The Ferrari rapidly disappeared round the bend with no panicky touch of the brake lights.

Far fewer tourists reached Inverloch, perhaps because access, except by sea, was finally by narrow Highland roads which had only received a superficial addition of tarmacadam since the days when Young Lochinvar rode his steed over them. Many of the inhabitants of Inverloch spoke Gaelic and when obliged to use the English tongue did so with a lilting West Highland accent, like the music of the sea lapping on a shore of shells. Looking back to his youth Cliff knew them as a gentle people, unhurried, and willing to speak to their cows, or pass the time of day with a stranger. He remembered the village dances — the girls occupying one end of the hall and the men, each with his half bottle of the 'createur' at the hip, occupying the other. It would still be the same, he felt sure, and still religiously terminate at ten minutes before midnight. And the Wee Free Meenister would still be the embodiment of God.

Tania drove carefully down to the bay round which the village had grown.

"Just look at that rock peak," she said, gazing at the great monolith of sandstone and quartzite. From the twisting mountain road they had just traversed it had looked like a cathedral roof with two gable ends. From below, one of these now reared up like a giant tooth.

"That's Stob Dearg, means the red peak. It's the western aspect of Bidean," Cliff told her.

"Is there any climbing on Bidean?"

"I reckon Lilly's route is the best line on this side. About 600 feet, Severe."

"You've climbed there yourself, then?" Tania arched her fine blond eyebrows interrogatively.

"A long time ago."

"I'd love to try it sometime. I've really grown out of langlauf and DHO's not for me."

"DHO?"

"Oh sorry," she laughed. "Ski prattle — down hill only. Look, isn't this our hotel? And look who's here before us."

In the car park of the Stob Dearg Hotel the yellow Ferrari with tyres the width of road-roller wheels and Turin number plates, lurked like a crouching grasshopper.

Two men were leaning on the counter at reception, chatting to the young woman hidden from sight in the office behind. They had obviously been patronising the public bar.

"They took that body away today, Morag," the voice was slurred and the gruesome tidings were punctuated by a loud hiccup.

"Aye, that's right," the second man affirmed, swaying slightly as if disturbed by the draught from the door through which Tania and Cliff had just entered. The first speaker, a lean gangly crofter, tried to light his pipe, but the point of ignition seemed curiously evasive. He uttered a Gaelic oath as he burnt his fingers.

"That sounds bad news," Cliff said, addressing the pipe-smoker.

The highlander looked at him from under craggy brows. "Aye, bad news, just. And when he was washed up they found his right hand was missing."

"That would be the lobster fisherman," Dempster suggested,

remembering the forlorn newspaper seller.

"That's right," the other man replied, exhaling a generous aroma of whisky. "But those chaps shouldn't be fishing lobsters with those snortles, or whatever they call them," he complained. "It's doing honest fishermen out of a chob."

"Losing a hand, though," Tania asked with concern. "That's very strange, is it not?" She looked from one man to the other.

"Vera strange indeed," replied the first man straightening up, triumphant sucking noises emanating from his pipe. "The police are thinking it must have been the screw of a boat that took his hand off."

"But no boat was reported in the area," the voice of the receptionist chimed in from the office behind the counter.

"No boat except his own," the second man replied, clearing his throat, "and that was anchored."

"What a horrible thing." Tania shuddered. "But I suppose lobster fishing is a dangerous sort of life."

Several miles to the north, a man wearing a thick tartan shirt was thankfully lifting the last of his creels.

Two more, a decent catch at long last. But he was unsmiling, the lines on his face hard while the mastoid muscle in his neck stood out like the powerful root of a buttress tree. He removed the lobsters from the pot. His large hands with blond hairs sprouting from the backs of the fingers were surprisingly deft. He was just about to replace the bait, as he always did before setting the pot again, when he stopped abruptly and stared as if mesmerised at something lying amongst the washed-up seaweed on a shelf of rock. He dropped the pot and used an oar to ease the boat alongside the rocky ledge. Very carefully, he balanced the object on the blade of the oar, retrieved it, and dropped it into the boat. Then he pushed off again, away from the rock, before examining his find.

It was a hand, severed at the wrist.

4

RHUDA ESTATE HAD been in the hands of the McBride family since the Battle of Largs in 1263. It extended over eighteen thousand acres, though the area itself was of little consequence, a bleak and barren deer forest. Two rivers bordered the estate on the north and south marches, both flowing east-west. The water of the River Bhan was let for an exorbitant sum to visitors who, fishing in good faith, seldom realised that the ghillie, who was so sympathetic and deplored their bad luck, had expertly netted the pool earlier the same morning.

At seventy-four years of age, Hector McBride didn't put much faith in the axiom that charity begins at home. He was not remarkable for his generosity. As lairds went, however, he was well enough liked. The Highlander accepts the laird as he accepts the minister, though the former may not have been installed by divine right. The occupation is not exacting. If the running of the Highland estate justifies paying a few men for the tilling of a patch of scree, then a factor is employed, a foreman whose uniform, unless it is a large estate and can run to a couple of kilts, is invariably tweeds.

There was no factor at Rhuda, just two gamekeepers. Alec Anderson and Johnny Anderson were not related and more commonly went by their nicknames, taken from the colour of their hair — one very dark, the other white. They were to everybody in Inverloch Alec Dubh and Johnny Bhan. The tourists called them the Black and White. The keepers knew the foibles of their master as well as they knew who took the twenty-pound salmon from the bridge pool over the Bhan the previous night.

The big hoose, as it was known locally, was a pretentious affair, and its owner would have found precious little excuse for throwing open the premises to the public, had he so desired, even for a token charge. McBride walked stiffly across the hall of his residence, where the stuffed head of a fine Royal spread its branches over an emaciated Kashmir rug. The knowledge that this particular stag had been shot on a neighbouring estate was a constant source of irritation to him. Several large paintings hung on the oak panelled walls, suffering from years of humidity and verging on saturation point. The paintings portrayed a long line of aquiline nosed, sharp featured McBrides. The present Laird's nose was also long and thin, like himself in fact; he resembled a drying rack onto which tweed and tartan garments had been thrown carelessly. It is common knowledge that there are fewer fat men in the Scottish Highlands than elsewhere, and the Laird was no exception. His skull seemed to have forced its way into a bag of skin which had subsequently shrunk.

"Good morning, James," he paused to address his son who was just descending the wide staircase. "Sleep well?"

"Thanks. As well as one can in this place. It's like Bombay in the monsoon, only fifty degrees colder."

"I think breakfast is ready," observed his father, choosing to ignore a remark which looked like leading to another fruitless family quarrel. It was early in the day to resume cudgels with his son. "I'll just take a stroll to ease my leg," he said, and selected a stout stick.

James McBride opened a door which led from the hall into the north wing. A further door on his right led into the breakfast room. His head felt like candy floss, and he noticed, without too much concern, a tremor in his hands. He told himself, without much conviction, that he had better eat. At twenty-nine James was over medium height, though not as tall as his father, and had developed a premature stoop. His light brown sandy hair was tending to thin at the temples and a lock hung down over his forehead, which he brushed back with a nervous gesture. He had been given an education which old McBride could ill afford — a good school with outdoor interests, favoured by royalty, followed by a rather mediocre degree at Cambridge. Various unsatisfactory jobs in the chemical industry had instilled in him a dislike for work, while a series of longish tours of duty to the Middle and Far East had promoted a liking for gin and drugs. His youthly interest in outdoor sports had withered and his physical appearance was now that of a young man impatient to enter middle age.

"Would you take porridge, Master James?" The accent was broad, the inflection disapproving. Agnes Chisholm, cook-housekeeper, glared with the severity of a sergeant major at the man who would always be young James to her. It would in her opinion be a sad day for Rhuda when young James took over. Agnes Chisholm presented a daunting air of authority with her ample-bosomed, white-overalled, square-rigged appearance, grey hair scraped back tightly over her head in a bun. Since the death of the Honourable Mrs Hector McBride eight years ago the running of the house had fallen entirely into her strong and capable hands. Agnes did everything, assisted by a Mrs McAskill who came in from one of the estate cottages part time to do a bit of cleaning.

Agnes's censorious features softened slightly as the third member of the family arrived. She approved of Miss Caren who was doing something useful with her life, nursing over at Raigmore Hospital, and coming home from Inverness at every opportunity to see her father.

Caren McBride burst into the room like a freshly scrubbed meteorite and greeted her brother and Agnes cheerfully. Her auburn hair, darker than her brother's, was cropped short. A small polished cairngorm hung from her neck on a gold chain. It had belonged to her mother.

"Where's old Gerry?" she demanded.

"Out for a wander," answered James. "Doing his mile run before breakfast."

"You shouldn't refer to your father as a geriatric, Miss Caren. It's not right."

"We'll all be like that one of these days, Agnes. He's lucky.

27

You should see some of my patients." She sat down at the large oval table opposite her brother, spread her napkin over her lap, and attacked a plate of porridge with a voracious appetite.

"There's coffee and tea, both freshly made." Agnes filled the toast rack as she spoke. "If there's anything else you need, I'll be in the kitchen."

"Thanks, Agnes," Caren smiled. "There's masses here for us."

"The master eats more than the both of you put together," Agnes replied reprovingly. "I'll have his ready for him as soon as he comes in."

"Any word of that university job you were after in Edinburgh, J?"

He looked up from his teacup morosely. "Not yet, but I don't think there's a hope. They're after someone who's had experience in lecturing rather than practical knowledge."

"I don't know why on earth you left that Calcutta post with those fertiliser people."

"Just that the boss didn't like the way I conducted my private life, as if it was any of his business. So I didn't sign on for another tour."

Caren studied her brother covertly under the guise of reaching for the marmalade to spread on her toast. He looked dissipated and listless and she felt sorry for him. It was probably being out of a job that made him moon around like this. James had been abroad on his last post for twelve months, then he had suddenly turned up four weeks ago and announced to his father that he was home for an indefinite stay until he found himself another job. Caren had always been very attached to James. They had shared their summer holidays, helping the keepers and wandering over the moors. It was great to see him once more, but at the same time she hoped he would soon find a suitable post and go away again. James and his father could not live peaceably under one roof, even a roof as accommodatingly extensive as Rhuda's. Last night had been a particularly bad row.

"Have you been talking to Dad about the estate again?" Caren glanced at her brother.

"Not again. You saw how he blew his top last time I broached the subject."

"I don't know why you are so keen to have him sell it. After all it's the only home we've got."

"We could buy twenty homes with what we could get from one of the oil companies," James spat back, his face flushing. "He's so damned stubborn. The place should be condemned, just look at that damp." He stabbed a finger at the ceiling where a large stain had spread from the outside wall. "And there's dry rot in the pantry and the kitchen."

"Oh, James, we went through it all a dozen times last night, and you know you won't get him to change his mind. Why are you so fierce about it all of a sudden?" It was the only topic that seemed to have animated her brother for the past few weeks.

James coloured briefly. "We're just damned lucky somebody wants to buy this pile, the state it's in," he muttered. "Only father can't see sense, as usual."

Hector McBride entered the breakfast room looking grey. The regular beat of his stick on the drive had heralded his approach. It sounded like a judge's gavel.

"Well, I must be off," said Caren, gulping down the remains of her tea. "Morning Pop. See you later." She couldn't face another scene like last night and James seemed to be smouldering towards one.

"Always in a rush, Caren?"

"My time off is valuable these days."

James looked up sombrely at his father. There wasn't much wrong with him physically, despite the heavy walking stick. The McBrides were well known for their longevity. A few arthritic aches and pains were but the rattles of a Model T Ford which still had a decade to run. The Laird returned his son's look with pale watery eyes which seemed perpetually focussed several days ahead. He sat down jerkily.

"Have you eaten?" He eyed the used cup beside the clean plate.

"Yes, thank you."

"The usual breakfast, Mr Hector?" Agnes stood stiffly in the doorway awaiting orders.

"Yes, please, Agnes. And another slice of bacon this morning. I'm a bit peckish. Almost a touch of frost today, James. But it may be good for a cast by evening if we get some wind."

A large bowl of brose was placed in front of the boney laird who proceeded to demolish it with considerable orchestration, arriving almost without pause at a clattering finale. During this interval James seized his opportunity. He felt wretched and prefaced his remark with a nervous look.

"You know, Dad, the Government could force you to sell Rhuda."

"Yes, by gad." The old man wiped his mouth with a large checkered handkerchief, the size of a competition chess board, then blew his nose as if heralding a cavalry charge. "They think they can force me to sell, but they've got another think coming. We've been here for generations, and I won't be pressurised by the blighters." He blew again, indignantly.

"They'll try compulsory purchase," James pointed out petulantly, laying aside a two-day-old paper he had picked up from the chair to help give himself an illusion of casualness.

"For some reason beyond my comprehension you want to sell your heritage, James." His father glared and shook his head sadly. "I had at one time high hopes for you and now you want to dispose of our family home. They'll build that refinery here over my dead body." His eyes glinted angrily and there was a wetness about them. His thin mouth twitched with indignation. He might have said more but for the timely arrival of Agnes, laden with a large plate of sausage, bacon and eggs. She placed the greasy creation in front of her employer with a flourish of her tea towel, giving James a triumphant sideways glance. McBride set to with fork and knife flashing, as though engaged in mortal combat. He didn't utter another word throughout the meal.

James McBride took his paper and himself out into the garden. His thoughts carried him back over the past weeks. It was amazing, he reflected, how things suddenly happened. By some perverse quirk of fate he had met up with Wilson again, and then there had been that letter with more than a hint of a threat about it. Blackmail might really be the more appropriate word. And it was not as if he had any conviction of his ability to deliver the goods. So how much did Paul Wilson know and, more to the point, what would he do?

"A bawbee for your thoughts." Caren's light voice fluttered across the anaemic lawn like the clear notes of a flute. "Come on, J, cheer up," she said more gently. "I wouldn't worry about the job. Something will come up, and until it does you can live very nicely on Social Security these days, Alec Dubh says."

"Thanks very much..."

"Oh, he wasn't talking about you, J. Actually, he's more concerned at present about that otter that's after the salmon in the river. He found two more dead today with lumps out of their backs, just behind the head. And did you know there was a chap drowned in Bhan Bay?"

"I heard."

"Supposed to have been lobster fishing," Caren went on with ghoulish relish. "But Alec thinks he was poaching. A boat ran him down in the night. Did you know he lost a hand? As well as his life, I mean," she added rather obscurely.

"That could have been a propellor." James endeavoured to summon a response. At least here was some poor beggar even worse off than himself.

"And they say nothing happens in the country," his sister concluded triumphantly. "Let's just hope things don't go in threes, that's all."

5

THE STOB DEARG Hotel had once been the ancestral home of an obscure Highland laird who had fallen, not by cold steel in the Jacobite uprising, but by prolonged encounters with the water of life, as the English language translates *uisge-beatha*. The grey turreted appearance of the three-storey building, with its roofs dressed in Ballachulish slate, gave the impression of a house in mourning, an effect accentuated by the black painted window frames and doors. Inside, some effort had been made to enliven a sombre interior by the removal of ponderous fireplaces, but the windows seemed to have been purposely designed to give audible and visible warning of the wind. Generous spaces between the sashes and frames ensured considerable turbulence during a north-westerly. In the 1930s, when the conversion to a hotel had been completed, central heating had been installed. The boiler room was located in the centre of the hotel, at a point where a small rectangular cemented area gave access from the rear of the almost square building. As the name of the installation suggested, the heating was purely central, for the pipes suffered constantly from blockages, which Archie, the handiman, blamed on the generous quantities of peat in the water supply.

From his room on the first floor Cliff noted that the harbour was busy. The *Celtic Pioneer* had come in since they had arrived, and several fishing boats were tied to the pier, while a larger and dirty foreign-looking trawler was moored, almost hidden, in the rocky bay at the northerly entrance to the harbour. There was some activity on the jetty where one of the boats was being unloaded and boxes of fish stacked onto a lorry. Gulls wheeled in tight circles, as if one wingtip were nailed to an invisible mast, voicing their impatience at the waste of good fish. Two small boys, their hunting instincts aroused, were intent on their fishing, ignoring the fact that the fishermen would give them fish far bigger than anything they could hope to catch with their joke rods. Skeins of mist floated across the face of Bidean, like ancient long ships. One could almost believe they had been hired by the Scottish Tourist Board for the late afternoon show, thought Dempster, as he turned to the mirror to shave.

In the empty lounge Tania ordered coffee from a waitress endowed with tree stumps in place of legs, and relaxed with a copy of *Scottish Field*. She was startled when a voice with a slightly foreign intonation broke in on her reading.

"You are a fellow guest, I think. May I offer you a drink?"

She glanced up in surprise. The speaker was in his late thirties and certainly, she decided, looked sartorially un-British. His dark trousers contrasted with an immaculate Italian-style white jacket, and he wore a loud red and yellow striped tie with his expensive silk shirt.

"Actually, I've just ordered some coffee. But thanks all the same." She smiled briefly to take off the firmness of the refusal.

"Ah, that is too bad. Perhaps later?" He hesitated for a moment and looked more closely at her. "If I am not mistaken, you are the charming young lady who passed me on the Ullapool road?"

"Oh, was it you in that fabulous sports car?"

"That is so," he acknowledged formally.

"Then, I'm afraid we were not ahead for long," Tania smiled. "You were just taking off, if taking off is the correct way of describing it?"

He was obviously flattered by her phrasing. "You drive well, for a woman."

"For a woman?"

"I have met very few women who can drive fast safely." He waved a graceful dismissive hand. "And even fewer who can drive fast at night. Can you judge distances at night?" He studied her teasingly, noting the fine line of her features, and the sweep of her neck above the soft white pullover.

"Well, I must admit that I'm not all that good at night driving." Tania fielded the question firmly and literally. "But I have no trouble during the day," she assured him, putting down her magazine as the laden tray arrived. The coffee was accompanied by a plate overflowing with biscuits and hot buttered scones. The waitress placed the tray carefully on the table, giving the man a sidelong glance.

"Here are your refreshments," he observed, "so I think I might have something too. A Cinzano, please, Kirsty." He flashed a smile at the girl.

"Yes, Mr Casini." She waddled off promptly.

"Would you mind if I joined you?" He gazed down at Tania.

"Why not?"

"Yes, why not," he repeated blandly, his eyes devouring her.

Well, she thought, that didn't take him long! Tania studied her companion covertly as he seated himself opposite her on a low chair. His features, she decided, could be described in a repertory company casting list as wickedly aristocratic. He had a certain attractiveness, undoubtedly, and if the looks she was receiving were any indication, he was no sluggard when it came to getting what he wanted...

"Oh, excuse my bad manners," he apologised and rose gallantly. "I neglected to introduce myself. Emile Casini, Sicily." He bowed slightly. Tania noticed there was an occasional clicking lisp in his speech, but his English was as good as her own.

"Tania Olsen, Norway," she responded.

"So, we are both strangers in an alien land?"

"Oh, I wouldn't say that," corrected Tania. "More like aliens in a strange land. Anyway, my forefathers pillaged this coast for five hundred years."

"So now you return with the olive branch?"

"That would be easier from your part of the world, Mr Casini."

"Touché," he replied smoothly. "Being Sicilian, I am gregarious by nature, I'm afraid," he confessed. "And interested in such a very attractive fast driver. What do you think of the Scottish Highlands?"

"Quite a contrast to London!" she smiled. "It really is enchanting."

"I agree with you. It is so peaceful and unspoilt."

"It's a long way for you to come on holiday, Mr Casini."

"Emile, please. For me it is part holiday, part business." He reached into his jacket pocket and produced a slim cigarette case. His gold lighter was shaped like a miniature racing car. "Yes," he continued. "I was hoping to do some fishing and hill-walking up here. I have to go on to Lerwick later. I am connected with the oil business, you see."

"That's a coincidence." Tania opened her eyes wide. "I work in London for Consolidated Oil."

"But how interesting. I believe they have some new establishment up here?"

"Yes, that's right. I haven't seen it yet, but it's due to be opened in a couple of weeks. A co-ordination centre. You must meet Mr Spencer," she went on.

"Also of your company?"

"A guest of the company. He's from UK Lubricants and is having a look at our set up. I'm here to show him around. Which company did you say you worked for?"

"I didn't." He smiled again. Tania found this constant smiling irritating. "Because I work for various companies." A spiral of smoke curled up gracefully from his cigarette. "Tell me, Tania — I may call you Tania? — will you be spending all your time taking this so fortunate Mr Spencer around your installations? Perhaps we can persuade him to give you what they call a day off. Then you can come out with me."

After a tryingly monosyllabic day with Cliff Dempster, the Sicilian's easy charm and frank admiration were balm to rebuffed feelings. Tania found herself warming to him and replied with more than usual vehemence.

"I'm quite sure he can do very well without me, and I should love a chance to get out in the fresh air and explore."

"Excellent. We could go hill-walking perhaps, or fishing if

you prefer. We could do much in the fresh air." Casini's eyes were assessing the knife-edge crease of Tania's trousers.

The conversation shifted to generalities about Tania and Dempster's immediate programme and to the length of time they were all likely to be staying in Inverloch. Casini's own plans seemed adaptable in the extreme. Tania concluded he was both bored with his own company and lonely and so far, she was obliged to admit, she had not seen the hotel bulging with female competitive talent.

Kirsty waddled back with Casini's Cinzano, blowing slightly. As she handed it to Tania's companion, her plain face graced by healthy ruddy cheeks, she simpered self-consciously. The Casini charm, Tania observed, had been cast wide. He obviously believed in keeping his hand in.

Dempster had changed into a sports jacket and a red cotton shirt. The Stob Dearg was scarcely luxurious, he decided, as he made his way downstairs, but it was functional, at least the carpets weren't tartan, and the staff appeared to be natives of Inverloch. He nodded perfunctorily to the receptionist, Morag, and went outside, and across the road.

Tourists' cars were parked at random along the sea-front road, as if cast up by a high sea. Several people perambulated gently and a few small boats were pulled up on the rock-strewn beach. To his left, further along the sea front, the *Celtic Pioneer* dominated the only jetty. The hydraulically operated jib of the gravimeter hung over the side, while two smart launches were suspended on davits from the foredeck. That gravimeter would be Wilson's pigeon, he decided, and wondered how soon they would meet. His eyes travelled back along to the red sandstone front of the hotel and he saw Tania emerge and look about her. When she saw him standing by the sea wall, she waved and came briskly over. The woman was taking her nursemaid duties seriously, he thought sourly.

"Ah, here you are." She smiled brightly, her hair wafted by the slight breeze. "I was wondering where you were." Dempster said nothing. "I've just met the owner of the Ferrari," she continued. "He's in the oil business too."

"Oh?" He raised his eyebrows slightly. "That could be interesting. One of you must have been quick off the mark," he added.

"He doesn't let heather grow under his feet," she replied equably.

"Tania!" A male voice boomed from further down the jetty. "If it isn't my own girlfriend come to keep an old man company."

Dempster saw Tania's face light up with genuine affection as they both turned to greet the newcomer. He was accompanied by a younger man of slighter build.

"Hello, Captain." Tania's voice held a good deal of warmth. "I was just going to suggest to Mr Spencer here that we stroll along and pay you a visit." She turned to Dempster. "This is Captain Alec Craig of the *Celtic Pioneer*."

Captain Craig put a bear-like arm round Tania and held out a hand to Cliff.

"Glad to meet you, Spencer. Hugh's the name, isn't it? Mr Swartze told me you'd be along sometime to have a look at the old tub."

"Glad to meet *you*, Captain." Dempster smiled down at this ebullient, friendly character. There were laughter lines about his eyes, but they remained the shrewd, assessing eyes of the seaman.

"Call me Alec. Not much formality in these parts. And this is Paul Wilson."

Over a drink in the lounge bar of the hotel Dempster had a chance to make his first assessment of the man Swartze had sent him to investigate. Paul Wilson, casually dressed in a mottled fisherman's jersey and blue jeans, seemed to blend inconspicuously into the upholstery. He was chatting casually with Tania, whom he had met on her previous visits, and nursed a Glen Grant in his two hands.

Alec Craig, who surprisingly drank nothing stronger than shandy, noticed the direction of Dempster's attention.

"Paul's our geologist," he explained. "He's the man that finds the black blood for us."

"Only one of many," Wilson protested modestly. "The Captain thinks I work with a divining rod." He gave a half-embarrassed ingratiating smile. Like an egghead Uriah Heep, Dempster thought, wondering how much ambition there was below the surface.

Captain Craig was explaining to Tania that the *Celtic Pioneer* was working quite close in at the moment. "In the morning we're going out, slightly south of here, to do a few jobs. Paul has to doublecheck some earlier survey work about ten miles away, just off the coast. Care to come down?"

Cliff deliberated for a second. "When are you returning?"

"Day after tomorrow. Be back here late afternoon, I would imagine."

"I noticed you've got a couple of launches on board. Any chance of borrowing one? We could cruise down the day you're due to return and see you at work, then get a lift back on the *Celtic Pioneer*."

"They'll have to leave in the launch about eight am if they want to see me in action," Wilson volunteered.

"Paul's doing some gravimeter stuff which might interest you, Hugh," the older man explained. "You can have one of the launches by all means. If you left at eight you should be down with us at the back of ten. It's not far down the coast. Past old Wilkins' platform yard and straight across Little Loch Broom."

It was agreed. The Captain promised to leave a launch for them at the jetty and claimed he had already personally organised a good weather forecast for the next couple of days.

Tania excused herself to go and change for dinner and the talk turned briefly to fishing out of deference to the decor. The bar was pleasant and unpretentious. Several prints of fish adorned the walls and an open peat fire blazed on the right of the door through which they had entered. Here, at least, one granite fireplace bore stout witness to the early Scots stonemasons. At the back of the bar, beneath the usual organ pipe display of inverted bottles, were two stuffed fish. Labels on them informed Cliff that they were respectively a brown trout of eighteen pounds and a salmon of forty-seven pounds. Talk of butchers, spoons, and casts confirmed Dempster's first impression of the group drinking whisky round the fireplace.

"Somehow you don't have the look of a fisherman to me, Hugh," observed Alec Craig. Once more the Captain seemed to read his thoughts with alarming ease. Dempster saw an opportunity for fishing of another sort and baited his hook.

"You're right. It's a bit too slow. But I wouldn't mind getting in some climbing while I'm up here."

"Ah, ha." Captain Craig beamed and wagged a finger at Paul Wilson who put down his whisky glass and looked at the big man with new interest.

"Well, I get up the odd Very Difficult from time to time," he admitted quietly, sizing Dempster up as he spoke. "And I can never find a climbing partner."

Their talk turned naturally and enthusiastically to the Alps and from there to the Yosemite Valley which Dempster knew from the dossier was where Wilson had had his accident. It was a part of the climbing world he knew well himself. Tania, arriving for dinner at that moment, thought dryly she had never seen Cliff's face so animated.

Her arrival signalled a general movement among the men. Captain Craig waxed enthusiastic over Tania's figure-hugging white cheong sam, and then trotted dutifully off to phone his wife. His son had been under the weather. Paul Wilson departed in quest of a brand of cigarettes Molly did not stock in the bar. Dempster bought Tania a dry sherry.

"Well," she took a careful sip from a brimming glass. Molly was generous with the measure. "Have you decided whether Paul Wilson is the villain of Consolidated Oil yet or not?" She spoke lightly, to disguise the fact that she was not yet entirely comfortable in the new cloak and dagger role Mr Swartze had thrust upon her.

"As a matter of fact, no. What I was just trying to decide at present was whether you wear anything under that dress."

Tania looked startled, then burst out laughing.

"A purely academic question," Cliff added, poker-faced.

"Well," her eyes danced, "for your information — not very

39

much." Her hand brushed his for a moment on the bar counter as they reached for their drinks. "But you don't really look like an academic."

Emile Casini appeared in the doorway. Erect and confident, his eyes swept the bar and came to rest on Tania. They also took in Dempster. He came smoothly across the room.

"Tania. Now I can buy you that overdue drink."

"That's very kind of you, Emile. I'd love another dry sherry. This is Hugh Spencer."

"I am pleased to meet you." Casini held out his hand. "Tania was telling me that you are studying the bones of the oil business."

"Sort of," Cliff replied unexpansively, returning the firm grip of the Sicilian. Casini's eyes were blue and chilly — negative, non-committal eyes, betraying no hint of the thoughts behind them.

"I must buy you a drink as well, Hugh. Molly!" He smiled at the girl who was pouring a drink at the other end of the bar. "Will you repeat the order here, please, and give me a Cinzano."

They moved to a table by a large window which overlooked the harbour. Casini admired Tania's dress. He admired the fine old clasp with runic markings on it which she wore in her hair. He admired the view. He admired Scotland.

"You will have seen quite a bit of Scotland by now, if you're in the oil business," Cliff ventured.

"There are plenty of oilmen around here, true," the Sicilian replied. "A few staying in this hotel, I believe. But I'm not really one of these heroes myself. I do a lot of the ground work for companies, a kind of go-between for subsidiary companies, that sort of thing." He gestured with charming vagueness.

"You must be working for Anglo-Italian, then," Cliff pronounced bluntly. The Sicilian raised an eyebrow. "It's the only other company with interest in the Thule field."

"I didn't say I was working *here*. My main work is in the Shetlands, with Arab-English International. But the fishing is not so good there."

"Or the climbing," Tania added, appraising the two men. There was a marked contrast between them. Cliff, large, precise and formidable; Casini, lithe, smooth, yet tough as rawhide. Molly came over with a tray of drinks.

"Ah, that is good of you, Molly." Casini was on his feet handing the sherry glass to Tania. "What is that you are drinking, Hugh?" He looked curiously at the second glass.

"Tomato juice and bitter lemon. A friend of mine calls it vampire bitters." The Sicilian rolled his eyes heavenwards in distaste.

"You climb?" Dempster inquired, as he settled back in his chair.

"In a modest way. I enjoy a bit of scrambling from time to time, and occasionally I put on a rope. Mainly to allay my fears."

"That's why most people rope up."

"You are a climber yourself, then?" Casini lifted his glass and smiled at Tania. "Cheers."

"I used to do a bit," Cliff admitted with careful diffidence. "But I'm decidedly rusty at the moment."

"We must get together one day," Casini suggested. "And polish you up again. It would be most enjoyable."

"Emile has promised to take me hill-walking, too," Tania told Cliff, slightly defiantly, "but I'd love to climb properly sometime. I've always promised myself a climbing course, but never got round to it."

"Here's another climber," said Cliff, raising an arm to Paul Wilson who had just re-entered the bar. He came over to their table and introductions were made. Dempster watched Wilson and Casini shake hands. They appeared to be sizing each other up, but it was impossible to tell what thoughts went on behind two equally impassive masks. Perhaps all oilmen got like this after a while. All that professional secrecy took a stranglehold on their systems, he thought morosely, and took up his observation post behind his glass.

"What a coincidence," Tania exclaimed, "to find three climbers in this tiny village."

"I'm sure we could include you as a fourth on an expedition, Tania. Don't you agree?" Emile turned to Dempster, who shrugged non-committally.

41

"She looks fit enough," Paul said, "but perhaps not in that dress."

Some of the guests were already assembling for dinner when Captain Craig came bustling over to the table. "Sorry, folks. I had trouble getting through. The tourists play hell with the telephones."

"Family all right?" Tania enquired.

"Yes, the missus always worries too much. Young Ian's just got a chill, but it's nothing really."

"Have you met Mr Casini, Captain Craig?"

The Sicilian stood up. "No, I haven't had that pleasure." They shook hands. Craig looked at him more closely. "Aren't you the chap with that yellow wedge of cheese outside?"

"You mean the Ferrari," Casini laughed.

"Ah, it's a car, is it?"

"What's the BHP?" asked Dempster.

"About 350. You are interested in cars?"

"Certainly. But I couldn't afford one of those."

"Tania, I've fixed up the launch for you," Craig said. "It will be all fuelled up ready, and I'll make sure there's one of those little gas stove contraptions so you can brew up if it gets chilly." They explained to the Sicilian about their plans for the day after tomorrow.

"Just one point," warned the Captain, "don't be tempted to land on that nice island off Gruinard Bay, will you?"

"There are plenty of warning notices to remind you," Paul Wilson reassured.

"But why not?" Tania asked.

"Anthrax," explained Dempster. "It's the place where the anthrax anti-toxin was developed, and the island's still infected with the spores. It's a pulmonary disease of some sort, if I remember rightly."

"That's it," put in Wilson. "If you were to be contaminated you'd have a faint chance of survival if you were able to take a massive dose of antibiotics immediately, but nobody I know's risked it to find out."

"So be warned," said the Captain. "It won't be free from

42

infection until the turn of the century. Gives me the horrors every time I pass."

"But that's appalling," cried Tania angrily. "Germs, military ranges and establishments everywhere..."

"And oil?" Paul Wilson added softly.

6

AFTER DINNER TANIA retired to her room yawning, overcome by the first soporific exposure to the balmy West Highland air. Outside her window the tide was almost turning and lapped gently at the beach below the road as Dempster let himself out of the hotel. He had forgotten what a Highland sunset could be like. It seemed to presage some miracle, a second coming, or at very least the North of Scotland Hydro Electric Board arranging the penultimate display of their resources. The entire west was aglow.

On the shore a man in a heavy sweater and waders, doubled down at the knees, was stooped over a net from which he was picking bits of seaweed with a concentration that made him totally oblivious of the strolling evening tourists.

Dempster leaned over the sea wall. "Can you help me, please?" he enquired, the tang of seaweed and tar strong in his nostrils.

"I can do ma best," was the even response. The fisherman removed a clay pipe from his mouth and straightened slightly. Not completely — the stoop was a permanent legacy of hard work.

"I believe a chap called Alasdair MacAlasdair lives here. Have you heard of him?"

"Well, now. There were two Alasdair MacAlasdairs from this village." The Highlander deliberated, taking another draw on his pipe. "There was old Alasdair and young Alasdair. Old

Alasdair died a number of years back, so I don't think it could be him you'd be meaning. He died round the point there in a bad sea, a fearful sea. He was told not to go out for his creels, mind — aye, by myself — but he had had a wee dram and he feared neither man, nor beast. Nor the sea." He shook a wise head at the folly of it.

"It must be the son, I think," said Cliff. "I seem to remember his father was drowned."

"Yes, yes. Young Alasdair. Ah, a wild lad, as bad as his father once. Now he was mad on fast motor bikes. Left here, let me see…" He spat with great accuracy at a rusty tin washed up by a high tide. A resounding ping acknowledged his marksmanship. After this punctuation he took another suck on his pipe. "Must have been about fourteen years ago. Aye, the years sail by, don't they?" The aroma of St Bruno, mingling pleasantly with the complex smells of the shore, reached Dempster now. "He was a great young lad, was Alasdair. He came back, of course, after his service in the Marines that would be. He was a Sergeant, you know. Yes, he came back after that, but he was restless. I don't know what made him take up with motor racing, but that's what he did. Doing well for himself too, until he had a smash in that big American race they have yonder. That's when he turned mechanic. He had studied the engines, you see."

"So you've no idea where he is now?" Dempster asked, straightening up with his hands apart on the wall, the death throes of the sun burnishing his face.

"Och, yes, yes, man. I was just coming to that. There's the trouble nowadays. Everybody's in such a hurry. He lives over there across the road in the second house. The one with the red window frames, you see? That's his boat down by the shore." He pointed with the white stem of his pipe towards a glass-fibre dory, pulled up above high water mark.

Dempster shot the man a suspicious look and then grinned broadly.

"You could have saved yourself the trouble of the history," he commented, "and told me where he was to start with. I used to know him."

"Well, well, now. I wouldn't have guessed that at all. Not at all." The fisherman picked up his net in the waning light and continued his examination as if it might be all of fourteen years before he would be asked another question.

At the latitude of 59°N it never becomes truly dark in springtime. It is as if the sun leaves a pilot light burning through until the next day — or until it next appears, since it tends to take days off in this land of rain and mist. It was as dark as it would ever be when Cliff knocked on the small door of Alasdair MacAlasdair's abode. The cottage rejoiced in the name of Tigh Bhan. This information was conveyed by a well-worn inscription burnt into the timber of the door many years ago. White House — not very original, but to the point. He knocked firmly on the door and the cottage echoed in protest. A large cobweb reinforced the top corner of the door frame above the hinges, as if there had been arachnidan misgivings about its structural strength.

Dempster hardly noticed the door swing open. There was no light behind and it must have been well-oiled. But then, if Alasdair MacAlasdair lived there, everything would be well-oiled and Bristol fashion.

"Looking for someone?" The voice seemed to come from a great depth.

"Alasdair?"

"Yes?" He could visualise the other's brain, running through its audio-visual file and trying to place him...no, no good. "Who's there?" Further information was evidently required.

"Cliff Dempster." A slight pause.

"Good God! What are you doing here?" Hands clasped together in the gloom, like two JCBs interlocking their buckets. "I thought you were dead, man, in Bolivia, or some such hole."

"Not yet," Cliff laughed.

"Come in, come in — what am I thinking about?" He switched on the lights. Alasdair MacAlasdair was a tall man, almost six foot, though he didn't look it, for he was solidly built. Blond hair, close cropped, made it easy to remember he had spent several years of his life in the Services. His most remarkable features, however, were his hands and arms. The

46

latter were massively thick, but his hands still seemed too large for the rest of him. They were enormous. But as many a top-rank mechanic knew, they were hands which could perform the most delicate operations at lightning speed.

"Pull that blind down, Alasdair. I don't want to be advertising my presence." In an instant Alasdair had the green blind drawn so that the cord rested on top of a china horse which guarded the window ledge with a glazed stare. The electric fire was on and a book lay open on the stool before it. Frazer's *Golden Bough*. He must have been finding it heavy going, for he had evidently been having a nap.

The interiors of most Highland crofts, Dempster had in the past found to his cost, were designed for Pictish dwarfs from a blueprint by Ossian. But he found that it was just possible to stand upright in what was obviously Alasdair's living room, with his head sandwiched between the black ceiling joists. The cottage was small but uncluttered. Whitewood panelling enclosed the stone walls. A flock of sheepskin rugs congregated in the centre of the floor. The furniture was simple and functional. Several pieces of china were displayed on shelves within a recess which had originally been a wall cupboard, while a twelve-day clock in a wooden case stood on the mantelpiece. Its bright brass pendulum belied the impression that time was standing still in this snug haven.

"Why didn't you let me know you were coming? And what the hell brings you here anyway?" Alasdair pushed forward a second comfortable easy chair and looked his old friend up and down with pleasure.

"To answer your first question," Cliff grinned, "I thought you were still with that racing stable, tweeking the double knockers. To the second, I'm on my usual run of business these days — officially studying the mechanics of making a fortune in extracting oil on behalf of UK Lubricants. Meet Hugh Spencer, nephew of old Sir Hubert Lamphrey, managing director."

"So, it's the usual intrigue and murder that brings you to the Highlands?"

"Possibly intrigue," admitted Cliff, crossing his long legs. "But not murder, so far."

47

"I wonder," Alasdair said softly. "John Pollock's body was found yesterday. I'll bet my last cent there's some dirty work there."

"Good God," Cliff looked startled. "Not Aqua John who used to be in the Unit?"

"The same. He had a couple of months free before he was due to take up an appointment with the Hong Kong police as chief underwater specialist. We were lobster fishing to pass the time."

"But what makes you suspicious?" interrupted Cliff. "I just can't believe Aqua John would *let* anybody bump him off. After all he was the sort of instructor who was the bee's knees at everything."

"It's a strange business." Alasdair suddenly sounded tired. "As I said, we were passing the time fishing. I'm down south now, but when John suggested a break I couldn't resist it, so we came up. I still keep the old house here for holidays."

"Wait a minute. Is this, by any chance, connected with that item in the newspaper about the death of a fisherman who lost a hand?"

"That's it."

"There was no suggestion of foul play in the press, was there?"

"Oh, it's a straightforward accident as far as the police are concerned." Alasdair reached for a bottle of ten-year old Talisker. He looked inquiringly at Cliff, who shook his head, before pouring himself a dram. His huge hands enveloped the tumbler.

"We had a sort of competition, you see. John was to dive for lobsters, while I was to use the conventional creels. The locals don't like people diving for them, you know. Not traditional enough, I suppose. It's the sort of experiment that's often talked about by inshore fishermen, but never tried. Anyhow, John was working in the bay to the north of me — Bhan Bay, where the Bhan river runs into the sea. You know the place, I think. The Old Man of Rhuda is that sea stack to the north of it, beyond the Rhuda lighthouse. I was fishing South Bay, just a mile north of here. His body was discovered by McPhail, the keeper at the lighthouse. It was washed up right under the cliff. His Gemini

— he brought it up with him for the holiday — was found anchored in the Bay. There's a very strong current running up the coast there, so one would expect a body to push off up towards the lighthouse, if he was fishing at Bhan Bay. His right hand was severed at the wrist and the airhoses cut."

"Carry on," Cliff said.

"I just heard today from the local John that the police surgeon's report indicated no further injury." Alasdair shrugged. "Officially he snuffed it from drowning, and the dismembered limb, as they phrase it, was probably removed by the action of the propeller. Similarly the airhoses. The police seem quite satisfied and the body has been sent down to East Malling for burial. But they're still looking for the boat that caused the accident." His last words were accompanied by a derisive laugh.

"What sort of boat would have been on the prowl at night?" Cliff watched his friend with some concern.

"Oh, plenty come in. Foreigners too. There's a lot of poaching within the limits, you know. The police have made inquiries, but so far nothing's come to light. Cliff, for God's sake, you don't honestly think that Aqua John would be thick enough to get caught up in a ship's screw, do you?"

"It does seem a bit incredible."

"Aye, too bloody incredible. There are a lot of incredible things about the whole business." Alasdair paused thoughtfully, rubbing his hand over a chin covered by a slight stubble. "You know A.J. had suspicions about something. There's a house at the Point over there which he was interested in." He waved a large hairy hand in the direction of the sea. "There's a nasty bit of work who's supposed to be the gardener. Now A.J. said this joker used to be in the Mafia in Spain. He came across him while he was out there on some unofficial jobs in the south, I gathered."

"A.J. used to be a bit of an expert on underwater harbour defences, didn't he?"

"That's right. Cliff, do you think he may have seen something he shouldn't when he was returning to Inverloch on the day of the night he was killed? Our routes back from the lobstering took us past the point each day. We were using separate boats."

"Didn't he give you any hint?"

"Not really — except a few days back he mentioned that he'd seen a chap diving up at the mouth of the Bhan."

"Oh? A local?"

"He wasn't close enough to see, but he thought it must be someone from the big house. It's called Rhuda. The river Bhan is part of the estate. Good salmon fishing."

"Well, I don't suppose there's anything unusual in someone diving, is there? After all, he was doing it himself."

"Aye, he was…"

"Was there something odd about the diver, then?"

"I just don't know," Alasdair frowned. "He told me he only saw him the once, but I don't think it's the sort of place where one would bother diving."

"What about salmon?"

"In broad daylight? No, that won't hold water. And there was no support boat, or anyone on shore either. As a matter of fact, I thought John himself was onto a bum steer when he dived there for lobsters. He had moved up from another small bay, just above South Bay where I worked. A lot of fresh water comes into the sea at the mouth of the Bhan, but somehow he was doing well enough."

"Perhaps it was young James McBride having a go himself?" suggested Cliff.

"So you know our local worthies, do you?" Alasdair looked at Cliff with respectful curiosity.

"I do my homework."

"The police arrived in the morning, just as I walked out this door. They knew he was staying with me. His Gemini was towed into harbour later."

"You didn't get the message when he failed to return that night?"

"Oh, you knew A.J. as well as I did, boyo. He liked to ferret things out on his own. He just went off about midnight, saying he was going to do some fishing. But he laid a particular emphasis on the 'fishing' bit of it. I wasn't going to interfere. I'm an honest tax-paying citizen these days."

50

"I suppose you're an elder of the kirk, as well?" Cliff chuckled, then asked more seriously, "Did he have his diving gear on?"

"Oh, yes, his suit. He carried the rest."

"What sort of an engine did he have in the Gemini?"

"A fifty hp Evinrude."

"That would have roused the slumbering populace."

"He didn't start the engine. He must have rowed out of Inverloch."

"Well, well," Cliff gazed abstractedly at the double bars of the fire. "You know, Alasdair, it's just possible that he did go lobster fishing. Did he have a torch?"

"Yes, he had a quartz halogen. The police didn't find it on the boat."

"So he could have been using the lamp at the time of the accident?"

"He could, yes."

"Anyone tried for lobsters at night before?"

"Not that I know of. Of course the police don't think Aqua was trying for lobsters at all. Oh, no. It was the salmon they were hinting at. Everyone here is salmon mad." Alasdair sounded disgusted. "They assume he was poaching, when another boat came in to net the river mouth and ran him down by mistake. I suppose that's been done before, too."

"Yes, it does seem to fit with what I remember of the poaching scene."

"True, but it doesn't fit John. Look, I was on a dozen risky jobs with him, and he was the most level-headed bloke I ever encountered. Even more so than you, though I don't often pay compliments to buggers like yourself." He smiled briefly. "I remember when he defused a new type of limpet mine off Valetta. It had been generously donated for active service from behind the Curtain to a certain Arab nation which bore us a grudge. Yes he was a cool customer, was John, very cool. I'm sure there was something niggling him, and he wanted to know more about it before he spilled the beans."

There was a pause, in which Cliff looked quizzically at his friend.

"You're playing your cards very close, Alasdair. I always know when you've something important to relate. You scratch your right ear. And you've done it three times in the last five minutes!"

"All right. I never could fool you, you bastard," Alasdair admitted grudgingly. "You always ferret things out with that nose of yours." He stood up, looking more than his thirty-eight years, and hunched through a door leading to the extension which had been built onto the rear of the cottage. Cliff heard a fridge door open, then slam, and the heavy tread as Alasdair returned. Silently, he dropped a black plastic bag on Cliff's knees and sat down again. Cliff lifted it and turned it upside down. A dismembered hand dropped onto his lap.

"That's the only part of John which didn't go back for burial."

"Where did you find it?" Cliff held it up, closely examining the section of wrist. Alasdair didn't answer, but handed his friend a powerful magnifying glass from the cupboard beside him.

"Have a shuftie with this," he urged.

"It's certainly a curved cut," Cliff admitted at length. "I suppose it must have been a boat's screw. Where did you find it?"

"On a shelf of rock in South Bay."

"I see." Dempster laid the hand on the floor on the plastic bag and glanced at his friend. "And the body was found — how far up the coast?"

"Five and a half miles, at the lighthouse."

"Was he still wearing diving gear?"

"Oh yes, there's a neutral buoyancy."

"Did you see the severed hose?"

"Aye, Charlie Galloway let me have a look at it when I identified the body."

"So it would be the right hand hose that would be cut, and the right wrist? If I remember, John always used a twin hose demand valve, didn't he?"

"Aye, I think so. But I don't know much about these aqualungs. I prefer to stay on the surface!"

"What was the cut on the hose like?"

"Looked as if it had been done with something sharp — I mentioned that to the Inspector."

"And what did he have to say?"

"Simply, that a propeller is as sharp as a bacon slicer when it has a few revs up."

"Yes," Cliff spoke with a faraway look in his clear eyes. "Air is fed through the right-hand hose to the mouthpiece and the demand valve is activated by the inhalation through the other. There wouldn't even be much air loss when the hose was cut. So, if he was run down by a small boat, it's quite possible that the occupants didn't see a thing — escaping air from a constant flow supply would have been a bit more obvious, even at night... I see what is worrying you, Alasdair," Dempster continued. "Hand in one direction; boat and body several miles up the coast. But why couldn't he have been run down in South Bay?"

"Then why was his Gemini anchored in Bhan Bay? Listen, I tried floating a small buoy at the same state of the tide as the night he was killed."

"From where?"

"The Point."

"And?"

"It was washed up within six yards of where I found the hand. The current carries flotsam up the coast to the north of South Bay, but anything going into South Bay stays there — it's been a beachcomber's paradise for as long as I can remember."

"So you think the hand was not severed at the time of drowning?"

"Either that, or the body was dumped further up the coast."

"Could be," Dempster mused.

Alasdair reached over and replaced the hand in its covering. He returned to the kitchen.

"A cup of coffee, Cliff? The water's hot."

"Please." A few moments later, Alasdair appeared, bearing two mugs. He placed one beside Cliff.

"Thanks — any foreign boats about just now?"

"Oh, there's always plenty out there." He pointed in the

general direction of the sea again. "Everything from Spanish, to Russian and Danish, I should think, but not many come into harbour. Only in bad weather. I think there were a couple of Norwegian shark fishing boats in the other day, and there was a Spaniard at the prawns. They usually work out in the Minch."

"You're not giving the hand to the police?"

"Not yet. The Fiscal isn't having a Fatal Accident inquiry — they seem to be treating it as death by drowning, and they think I'm just scare-mongering. I had a word with the Procurator Fiscal this morning, in Dingwall. I've known him for years — we went to school together. He only said, 'Even Commandos have to die, Alasdair.' But I bet they'll do their damnedest to find out if a boat was in Bhan Bay that night."

"And how long will that take?"

"A bit of time. The white fish boats won't be in till the weekend. But it's just possible one of them might have noticed something on its way out last weekend."

"Are there any other lobster fishermen about here?"

"No, it's been more or less fished out — prawns and clams are what they're after now." He poured himself another half tumbler of the rich malt.

"What else did A.J. say to you about that diver up at the Bhan?" Cliff pursued his train of thought.

"Nothing much. I think he mentioned the gear the other chap was using looked like re-breathing equipment, but he wasn't sure. Whoever it was surfaced some distance away, apparently, in the mouth of the river."

"I see," Dempster replied with increased interest. "Well, one thing we can do Alasdair. Will you take that hand round to the Western Atlantic first thing tomorrow morning? There's a helicopter pilot supposed to be staying there. Name's Jim Atkinson. He's meant to be on hand for me — for Hugh Spencer, that is. He can take it down to Inverness for the London flight. I want a lab to eyeball that parcel as soon as possible."

"Atkinson, right."

"I'll give him a ring to fix it and contact the boffins at the lab."

"Well, we're all STD up here now. No tittle-tattle. Highland gossip's been reduced fifty per cent since the change-over. Where are you staying? The Stob Dearg?"

"Where else?" Cliff drained his coffee mug and stood up, remembering to avoid the beams. "I'd better be on my way back there."

"You're not shrinking, that's one sure thing," Alasdair laughed. "But are you still as weak as ever?"

"I could pin you, at any rate, you lazy slob," Cliff grinned affectionately.

"Aye, you did the once — when I was off colour and looking the other way. Nobody's done it since."

"Not much opportunity for dangling your dainties these days, I imagine. All oil flushing and bumf filling..."

"Oh, I still keep fit, lad. Don't try me."

"A.J. wasn't married was he?" Dempster asked.

"No. But his mother's alive still. I've written, and done something about flowers. No wife and children, though." They moved toward the door.

"And how about yourself?"

"Not now. Lost my wife and kid in a car crash. I was out at the Brickyard at the time," Alasdair said shortly.

"I'm sorry."

"I've got a couple of garages down south nowadays."

Cliff followed the lead of the change of subject. "The heap I've borrowed for this trip might interest you. Two-litre Lotus in a four-wheel-drive Mini!"

"Oh? Who was willing to spend money on that kind of half-breed?"

"Swartze, the big boss of Consolidated Oil."

"So you're working for him?"

"Consolidated want Rhuda for a refinery."

Alasdair whistled silently. "And old McBride?"

"He won't sell."

"I'm not surprised. He's part of the landscape."

"Looks as if another company could be in the running for the site, as well. So keep your ears open for me."

"I'll do that. Nothing like a semi-resident ear in the gossip pipeline. Now I think of it, I fancy I heard that house out on the Point has recently been bought by an oil concern. Anglo-Italian, something like that."

"Indeed? And that's where A.J.'s Spanish Mafia character hangs out, too?"

"Sort of coincidence, do you think?" asked Alasdair hopefully.

"Here's another one. You noticed that yellow Boxer yet outside the hotel?"

"Yes, quite a heap. I wouldn't mind one myself."

"Well that heap is owned by one, Emile Casini, and he works for several foreign oil companies, possibly even Anglo-Italian Oil."

The two men stood in the porch, with the cottage door held close against the light. Into the speculative silence Cliff said, "I think I'm going to be around for a while, Alasdair. What about you?"

"I'll be here, if you need me. Fishing — you know."

"Hmm. We'll both be."

7

TRIGGER MACKAY GLANCED at his watch and observed that it was midday precisely. He was walking along the only street in Inverloch, his hands motionless and held slightly away from his hips. He was daydreaming. *High Noon.* Now that was a good film. His hands twitched convulsively. Pity they give the impression of six gun accuracy in these films, though...

PC MacKay had earned his nickname because of his obsession with firearms. It was not that he enjoyed using them, quite the contrary. Living in the heart of the Highlands, he would have had ample opportunity to go out with a dozen or more game-keepers when they shot to cull and replenish the estate's larder and exchequer. There was no belly-crawling, arse-waving nonsense when they shot; they just took the Land-Rover out when the snow was down, and collected more beasts in one morning than the 'veesitors' and gentry did in a season. No, Trigger liked the guns themselves, not what they could do — all kinds of guns, from Army 25-pounders, to micro-bore pistols. They were all grist to his ballistic mill. With due respect for this affliction — for the policeman who dreamt of being a sheriff — the head keepers of the larger estates would set aside a full day for Trigger's firearm inspection, a task which any normal member of the law would have concluded within ten minutes, inclusive of a dram or two. But, with many a 'tut-tut', inevitably Trigger would find a speck of dust in every breech and remove it as if it was the spore of a deadly fungus settling in an open

57

wound. For a few delirious months, he had worked at Head-quarters, and been in charge of receiving and cataloguing firearms returned during an amnesty. This had proved one of the highlights of Trigger's life, although the subsequent disposal of these revered possessions in a deep and distant part of the North Sea, whilst a belligerent senior officer supervised, had caused him acute distress. But his present job was as good as any. After all, there were the visitors who came up for the stalking, and there were sometimes complications with their weapons, usually expensive, and certainly a joy to behold.

"Morning, Jim," Trigger addressed a pair of legs sticking out from under a Cortina. The legs were clothed in overalls he recognised as belonging to the proprietor of the Western Isles garage, one James Dalrymple. "Can you tell me what spare parts you've sold for outboards, Jim? Just a routine check?"

"Oh, that poacher. Nope, I've not sold a thing. And I can tell you something, Trigger: if he lost his hand on an outboard prop, then the owner wouldn't be buying his spares here. It wouldn't damage it much anyway."

"Just checking, Jim. We'd look pretty stupid if you'd sold a new screw to someone, wouldn't we?"

"Aye, I suppose so, but don't you think I'd have tipped you off?"

"Yes, I suppose you would at that."

"Your Panda is due for service tomorrow, remember?" Jim wiped his hands on a dirty cloth.

"Aye, you can keep her for a few days, if you want. I could do with putting some mileage on my own buggy just now, and I'll have to use it if the police car's in dock. I'll soon be off on holiday. Just got a mileage increase," he added as an afterthought.

As county police go, Trigger was competent enough. He had been in Inverloch three years now, and knew all the trouble-makers — not that there were many. 'Spooner' Cochrane, his predecessor, had given him a run-down of the district in a succinct half hour. Spooner had been sorry to leave — a rabid fisherman, the weather just couldn't be too wet for him.

Trigger seldom arrested anyone, believing prevention was better than cure. If a poacher was overstepping the mark, he would simply drop a casual hint to a friend that he would be 'paying a visit' one of these nights. This generally had immediate, if not lasting, results. The deep-sea fishermen could cause trouble though, and the Norwegians, when they came in, made a bloody science of getting drunk.

Back in Headquarters a meeting was just concluding between Detective Inspector Charlie Galloway and his Chief, Mr Orr. Mr Orr, MBE, LLD, was a quiet man and lucky to have been accepted when he joined the force thirty-two years ago. At barely five foot eight he had had the dubious distinction of being reckoned the shortest policeman in Scotland at the time.

"So, Charlie. There's not too much doing in your half of the moor?"

"Not a great deal sir. The Larbh Hotel investigation is well under way. We had a tip off that it was the Paisley gang and Strathclyde will pick them up, if we don't."

"Good."

"Nothing yet from Inverloch about that Marine chap. PC MacKay, the Inverloch one, sir" — there were four different MacKays in the division — "told me that the Spanish trawler has gone. She was about before the Bhan Bay fatality."

"Did you question the crew?"

"Oh, I had a word, as best I could with the Customs man from Kyle as interpreter, but they seem to be in the clear. Their boat's too big for the dismembering job. Doc Allison thinks it was probably a big outboard with a plastic propeller."

"Well, keep your eyes open, Inspector. Something may turn up yet."

"Right, sir."

Detective Inspector Charles Galloway had joined the force as a young man in Glasgow. Few places offer a tougher testing ground than the Mean City and, understandably, he had grown into a fair but tough cop. He had discovered at an early stage in his career that the Scottish criminal is unique and as hard-headed as a boiler-plate rivet. It is seldom that you hear him ask for other previous offences to be taken into consideration, as they do down south.

Charlie was a popular man. He played fullback for the local soccer team and was a dab hand at the shinty. The involuntary grimace as he rose to leave his chief's sanctum was the result of too violent contact with a stick. What came of playing the Glen Merag team after putting two of their members away for six months.

But it was not shinty which occupied his mind that morning. It was the decease of Sgt. Instructor John Pollock, RM. He had inspected the locus. It all seemed obvious enough. Similar accidents had happened before and, he thought gloomily, would happen more frequently as diving became more popular. But the man had been no fair weather, once-a-week diver. He was a professional, possibly one of the best in the country. And in Charlie Galloway's mind there were some niggling doubts which had been irritating him ever since. The man's ex CO had written, 'I find it hard to credit that John Pollock has met his end in this manner, unless crippled by a heart attack, or some other agency…'

'Some other agency' — that chap MacAlasdair had said much the same. He wondered about MacAlasdair. Supposed to have been Pollock's oldest pal. No obvious motive. But Charlie was a good policeman and was paid to be suspicious. Yet again his mind went over the sequence of events and known facts. Johnny Bhan's wife had thought she heard an engine out in the bay that night sometime after three when she woke to let out the cat. It could have been a fishing boat, of course, or Pollock's own boat. Or the boat that carved him up. The suggestion that the man had been diving for lobsters was not too fantastic. Charlie had dropped a creel or two in his time and conceded that night fishing might have possibilities. He didn't believe Pollock had been poaching — not a sign of a salmon scale anywhere, and no gear even remotely suitable in the inflatable. But it would be convenient for the time being to leave the impression that this was the official line of thought, and that the matter was closed. Poaching was a delicate subject, and it would be some time before word filtered through of recent happenings. Charlie was determined to find out what boat had been in the bay that night, but he was prepared to bide his time. It was more than likely the

60

crew never even knew they had run Pollock down — a tiny pause in the regular rhythm of the screw and away again. Or they might have found him, hand and all, among the salmon in their net.

When Alasdair lifted his creels that morning he only found three lobsters. On impulse he decided to move them up to Bhan Bay and round Rhuda Stack. He had twenty creels in all, and they were soon hauled and piled on the dory. He took the boat slowly, for it was a top-heavy load. He knew it would be a bit further to go each day, but what the hell? It was pleasant out in the boat — and bugger all else to do. He would try some of those limestone rock pockets at the mouth of the Bhan, despite the fresh water from the river. He enjoyed the trip up the rocky coast; the gulls squealed at him and he saw a Great Skua winging its way on its headland beat. Easing in close in the quiet water, he dropped ten creels at six fathoms, marking them with four buoys. He looked back in satisfaction at his new family of orange heads, before setting off towards the Stack. Inchmhor Island lay on his left, like a sleeping caimen; ahead was the Rhuda breakwater. A solitary figure stood at the very extremity of it; as he drew closer he saw it was a girl. He throttled down and kept in close.

"Early bird, catching worms?" he shouted as he came slowly alongside her.

"Well, what next? A punning lobsterman," she laughed. "Where are you going?"

"Up to the Stack — want to come?"

"Why yes," she sounded surprised. "If you're not going to be long. I was just enjoying the salt air."

"About forty minutes, I should think," Alasdair took the boat alongside so that she could jump aboard.

"You're Mr McBride's daughter aren't you?" He looked up at her with interest.

"Yes... Do I know you?"

"Alasdair MacAlasdair from Inverloch — you do now!"

"My name's Caren. Pleased to meet you, Captain." He indicated that she should sit on the oilskins on the transom. She

61

was used to boats, he noted, and moved with confidence in her blue jeans and hand-knitted pullover.

"I thought maybe you were a siren when I first saw you standing there!" Her blue eyes shone and she laughed with a natural ease which suggested that she laughed often.

"I'm just a plain bandage and bedpan nurse," she admitted. "Alas, no siren... You know, you don't look like a fisherman." She surveyed him critically: strong features and tanned face, tartan shirt open at the neck, and his hands — she had never seen hands like those.

"My father was a fisherman, and his father before that."

"You haven't answered my question," she pouted good-humouredly.

"Well, let's say I do it part-time." He looked ahead to where the skerries were strung out, like probing fingers reaching for Inchmhor.

"Any luck with the lobstering?"

"So-so. They seem to be scarce just now. I've just dropped ten pots at Bhan Bay, and I'll put the rest down at the Stack. Might have better luck there." They rounded the skerries and the top of the Stack became visible: a coastal phallus of Torridonian sandstone.

"Did you hear about that man who drowned up here? People say he was poaching of course. But everything gets blamed on poachers in these parts."

"Yes, it does." Alasdair spoke shortly.

"What do you think?"

"He wasn't poaching, Caren. I can assure you of that. John Pollock was one of my best friends."

"I'm sorry," the girl said quickly. "I shouldn't listen to gossip..."

They were both silent until they came in closer to the Stack and Alasdair eased the throttle back. The water was deeper here, and the cliffs three hundred feet high, the height of the pinnacle itself.

"I used to walk up here when I was young and just stare at it," she remarked pensively, gazing at the red tower. "It used to fascinate me — still does! Has it ever been climbed?" She

62

transferred her gaze from the Stack to Alasdair and, for an instant, saw some similarity — a look of indestructability: solid bone and muscle on one hand; solid rock on the other.

"Oh yes, it's been climbed all right, but not very often — it's hard."

"It looks quite impossible," she replied, craning her neck.

"I think I'll put a couple of creels down here." Alasdair peered into the soft, green depths. "But God knows what'll happen if a sea comes up — I'll be in trouble then!"

"Can I help?"

"Well... You could pass them back to me — that one on the top right to start with, or the lines may get fankled. And watch your clothes!"

"Goodness," she remarked, amused. "You're worse than matron!"

Twenty minutes later, they were all set to his satisfaction. Heading well out, they sped back down the coast. The boat planed smoothly at twenty knots, with the punch of a 50 hp engine behind it, and conversation was impossible. Approaching the breakwater, Alasdair slowed down and drifted gently inside to the steps.

"Hmm that was superb!" Caren said. "Can I come out with you again?" She stepped out of the boat.

"Sure; any morning, and most evenings."

"I'd like to see if we've caught anything — I love lobster!"

"Take this one here," he handed her a large lobster from his morning's catch.

"Can you spare it?" she enquired anxiously.

"Sure — we'll have hundreds tomorrow!"

"Thanks, Alasdair," she collared it expertly.

"Probably see you tomorrow morning then — unless it's blowing a force 9. I may come, even so!"

"I hope so," she laughed as she alighted. He took the dory astern, opened the throttle, and sliced past the breakwater into the open sea, then waved nonchalantly back to her.

8

THAT SAME MORNING Cliff and Tania drove over to Consolidated Oil's new co-ordination centre, so that Hugh Spencer could be seen to be paying his respects by anyone who wanted to look. Tania assumed her guided tours voice and explained the function of the new building.

"It's mainly a land communication base for the platforms in the North Atlantic," she explained. "We have one there at present, supplied from Kyle of Lochalsh. Anglo-Italian's platform is the only other one in the area, with its land base at Kyle too. The Centre will mastermind communications along this coast for us."

"Not the handiest spot to get at, is it," Cliff observed dryly.

"Not yet. But the main road south to Ullapool is only a few miles away, and the County Council are supposed to have promised to drive a double track road to the Centre later this year. But it's got its own helicopter base, of course, for personnel transport and light freight, that sort of thing. Talking of which, that's the hotel where the pilot, Jim, is staying. The Western Atlantic." She pointed to a substantial stone building perched grimly on a headland, to all appearances still suffering from the hangover of the previous winter. "The food is supposed to be excellent," Tania volunteered dubiously. After passing the Western Atlantic they nosed inland through desolate country and at the top of a rise, just past a crossroads, had their first sight of the Centre. It had only very recently been painted white and it dazzled the eye. A fine low building of pre-stressed concrete and cedar wood, its large windows lent it a rather clinical spaciousness. The main entrance faced north. On the left was a large carpark, while the other side was flanked by long storage buildings with high doors. A helicopter squatted on the rear of the roof. The main concrete heliport extended from the side of the store buildings — a large expanse of compomat, a windsock and antennae mast were to the rear, where the fence marched with the open moorland on the southern side.

They were shown around by a tallish tweedy young man who gave Dempster a momentary twinge of anxiety when he cheerfully announced that he too had worked for UK Lubricants some years ago. "I gather old Sir Hubert is feeling his age a bit these days?"

"Well, he still gets about, you know," Dempster answered carefully. "But sometimes requires the assistance of a stick."

"Aye, none of us is getting any younger, that's certain." The young man led the way through an array of packaging debris. "I was told you'd be over later in the week to have a look at the office arrangements, Miss Olsen. It's like a film set at present, I'm afraid," he apologised. "Wire, paint, and plaster. There's been a hold-up with electronic components — seems to be a hold-up with everything nowadays — so it's doubtful if they'll get the signals wing completed before a week Wednesday. I'll just show you the way up onto the roof now. Jim Atkinson should be up there and I'll hand you over to him, if you don't mind."

Beyond the main entrance areas, close to the stairs which they ascended, a group of painters were working with unusual alacrity for the British, suggesting a piece-work rate. But they still found time to devour Tania with their eyes, as if she had just stepped out of a Pirelli calendar. Their guide left them in the roof doorway.

The handgrip of Jim Atkinson, Swartze's crackerjack helicopter pilot, was firm and friendly. He was a dark, lean man with a reckless grin, though in his job he was probably the safest man Consolidated Oil employed, or indeed, any other company in the north, where good pilots are as plentiful as black-backed

65

gulls. He greeted Tania with a hug and a kiss. She responded in kind, but cried out in mock alarm.

"Hey, you fool. You'll break my ribs. I'll have to get my bodyguard to deal with you."

"Well, girl," Jim drawled, releasing her, "I guess your body does need guarding. Glad to meet you Spencer. I've done that delivery you phoned about so bright and early."

"What's all this," Tania asked, her eyebrows raised.

"Just delivering a parcel to Inverness airport from me this morning. And thanks very much." He turned from the pilot to Tania. "I forgot to mention it."

"Forgot my foot…" Tania bit her lip, but said no more. Cliff had let her prattle on about the hotel where Jim was staying while he had already been in touch with him up to some cloak and dagger ploys which he obviously had no intention of telling her about. She realised that up to now she had thought of herself and Cliff Dempster working together as a team, for no better reason than that she wanted it to be so. Clearly he felt differently. She was flushed with hurt and anger. Jim Atkinson was telling Cliff about the new Lama and its long range fuel tanks.

Cliff smiled and regarded Tania quizzically. "You should be cross more often. It's awfully becoming."

The afternoon had been dedicated to a possibly more fruitful social call at Rhuda. Tania was still smarting from the morning rebuff and Dempster appeared to feel no need to fill the conversational void, so they travelled most of the way in silence.

As they drove up the road leading to the estate grounds, a high boundary wall ran in either direction; on the right, it followed parallel to the road for some way, the left-hand branch terminated on the rocky beach over a mile away. Passing between scattered trees, the rough drive took them close to a small keeper's cottage, nestling beside the river Bhan. As they slowed to rumble across a bridge of wooden planks Dempster noticed how low the water was.

Rhododendrons were plentiful at Rhuda, but had evidently been once regimented into orderly clumps, not left to bloom in the careless profusion seen on many a West Highland hillside. There was surprisingly little mature woodland for an estate of its size, apart from the Caledonian pines and a few silver birches sheltering the house. But the elegant sweep and extent of the lawns, although now unkempt, bore testimony to the former glories of the estate.

The house itself reared up, an impressive bulwark of Torridonian sandstone. On closer inspection the window frames were badly in need of a coat of paint. The grass around the house had been rough cut, and the green sward stretched away to the shore where a stone jetty reached out into the sea.

"Look," gasped Tania, breaking the silence.

By the Gibbs surround to the front door stood a tall, angular man in a kilt, heavy Harris wool stockings and brogues, and a faded green tweed jacket. He grasped a crook for support, or possibly to repel the Mini at which he was glaring contemptuously.

"That is just exactly how I've always visualised a real Highlander," breathed Tania. "The Laird himself."

"Either you or he has been watching too many whisky commercials."

They walked over to where McBride was standing and Cliff made the necessary introductions.

"Hugh Spencer, eh," the forbidding look lifted slightly. "Yes, Lamphrey wrote and told me you might call. Very good of you. Come in, come in Miss Olsen. So you're Marilyn's son, aren't you? Don't think I've met you before. Perhaps when you were very tiny." The Laird chuckled to himself. "And that would have been a very long time ago." He looked keenly at Dempster. "You're not like Hubert," he barked, "not as flabby looking. But that's no bad thing." He chuckled his dry chuckle and recollecting his social duties ushered them indoors. "Come in now. In here Miss Olsen. Agnes is about to serve tea."

"Oh, we don't want to impose on you, Mr McBride," Tania said quickly. "You must be awfully fed up with people pestering you in this lovely spot."

"Yes," McBride agreed, as he moved to the door, limping slightly. "Tourists and midges, between them they spoil the

Highlands. Meet the family," his voice resonated as he led the way into the large drawing room.

A young woman who had been writing at a delicately ornate desk stood up and came over to be introduced. A spare, nervous young man stood by the fire. "Caren, my daughter, and my son, James. Miss Tania Olsen and Hugh Spencer. Er, Hubert Lamphrey's nephew."

His perfunctory introductions concluded, the Laird left Caren to chat and organise the visitors into chairs. James McBride nodded briefly, but showed no further interest then, or when the door flew open to admit Agnes, carrying a laden tray. She glared at Cliff and Tania, and turned accusingly to Caren.

"No-one told me there were to be guests!"

"Oh, it's all right, Agnes," Caren soothed. "Just another couple of cups, please. You've enough on that tray to feed an army!" Agnes sniffed and deposited the food on a Benares table near the fireside. James moved even closer to the fire and stood with his back to it.

"Your house has a superb situation," Cliff observed into the silence of Agnes's wake. Tania privately enjoyed the spectacle of her companion obliged to make polite conversation.

"I never get tired of it my boy," McBride boomed. "Now sit down and tell me about Hubert. Saw quite a change in him last time, and he's younger than I am. That City life's the trouble. It warps both mind and body."

"Well, with all due respect sir," Cliff eased himself into a ruptured armchair, "he does still get about."

"Yes, yes," the Laird echoed impatiently, as if he had a monopoly of mobile old age, "but I haven't regretted ignoring the City. This is the tempo of life that suits me."

Caren had been ascertaining Tania's nationality and enquiring how she liked Scotland.

"I love it," her guest enthused. "And out here the Atlantic looks so vast, and the houses so, so — "

"Damp?" enquired Caren's brother, his tanned face almost yellow in the firelight.

"Don't listen to him," Caren smiled. "James is used to working in more tropical parts and doesn't like our climate."

"It's just the eight months which are wet each year that I don't like. The other four aren't so bad, but Rhuda resembles a sponge, you must admit."

"Oh, come on James." Caren could see the drift of her brother's thoughts and hoped he was not going to treat their visitors to another instalment of the family row. As a diversion she began placing cups and saucers on small side tables with more busyness than was altogether necessary.

Cliff had been trying to size up James McBride. Despite his tan, he looked unwell, with the air of one who has spent too long propping up bars. His fingers were slender, like his sister's, but they shook. At that moment Agnes stormed in with more china and a large plate of superfluous buttered scones, and left with a satisfied smirk. The serious business of consuming afternoon tea began.

McBride quizzed Dempster with disturbing persistence on the precise nature of the younger man's role in his friend Sir Hubert's company, and Cliff found to his cost the Laird was not a man to accept a hedging answer. The conversation then naturally turned to Scottish oil in general and the iniquities of the developers and the big corporations, which seemed to be legion. At the end of the catalogue Dempster ventured, "Well, I'm glad UK Lubricants doesn't have any holdings in Scotland. I'd be scared of being lynched!"

"You sound as if you've spent some time in America, Spencer?" The Laird looked sharply up at Cliff.

"I was born here in Scotland, sir, but I have lived in the States and in Tahiti for some time now."

The reference to Tahiti produced an envious sigh from Caren, and in order to avoid being asked about an island about which he knew very little and liked less, Cliff decided to turn the conversation into other possibly more informative channels. "Are *you* in favour of this oil bonanza?" He addressed himself to James McBride. Immediately, he sensed an atmosphere, but the tension in the room came from Caren McBride not her brother. She relaxed again, however, when James stared judiciously at Cliff over the rim of his cup and said, "Not the way it's being done."

"Oh?" Cliff raised an eyebrow. "How's it being done that you don't agree with?"

"Well, that platform yard down the coast looks bloody awful for a start."

"But that won't be there permanently," Cliff pointed out, "once they've finished building and are away drilling."

"Oh, the drilling aspect is interesting all right." James's attention for once was engaged. "Tell me, do you know how they change the direction of the drill when it's a few thousand feet down?"

Cliff laughed deprecatingly. "You shouldn't ask me. I'm up here to find out that sort of thing. I'm new to the business. You should meet a chap we were introduced to last night called Paul Wilson." He watched the heir of Rhuda from under slightly lowered eyelids. It was hard to decide whether he had paled under the tan.

"The factor up at Glenusher is a Wilson," James turned away to put his cup with exaggerated care on the mantelpiece. "But I don't think his name is Paul, is it, Dad?"

The Laird who had been massaging his knee vigorously, heaved himself to his feet and limped stiffly to the window. "No." he said, "his name's Duncan."

Cliff pressed on. "Paul Wilson's a geologist on the Consolidated Oil survey vessel, *Celtic Pioneer*. He could supply you with all the scientific answers. The boat's been in and out of Inverloch lately. Perhaps you've seen it there?"

James was saved by his father's wrathful observation of the first midges of summer. "Look at them," the old man waved a bony finger at a dancing cloud beyond the glass. "They're out even at this time of day and at least a month earlier than usual."

"I was reading about your midges recently." Caren looked up fondly at her father.

"Not in a Scottish Tourist Board handout," her brother observed dryly.

"It's mainly — let me get this right — Culicoides impunctatus we have round here apparently, and it's the female that bites!"

"I liked that impunctatus bit," said Tania later, as they drove away from the house. "Well, what do you think of the heir of Rhuda? Why do you think he made such a thing of not knowing Paul?"

"I don't know the answer to that one — yet," Cliff mused, "but," he added with force, "I can tell you one thing. James McBride is a hophead."

9

THE HOTEL WAS getting busier daily, but few of the guests had surfaced by the time Tania and Cliff had finished an early breakfast next morning.

McCallum, the proprietor, emerged from his office as Morag left Reception to go in quest of the couple of packed lunches that had been ordered the night before. "Good morning, Miss Olsen, Mr Spencer. You're off with the launch today? Now, you know which way to go? Captain Craig said he'd be down off the south end of Gruinard Bay. You'll have no trouble finding them — just head straight across Little Loch Broom. Take you about two hours, I reckon." They made a handsome couple McCallum thought enviously. Lucky sod, Spencer, though he seemed to take the girl very much for granted. Maybe her type liked it that way? He wondered lingeringly what she was like in bed.

Morag returned bearing a bulging plastic carrier with a colour reproduction of a Highlander in full regalia emblazoned on its sides, and McCallum was obliged to switch his welcoming spiel onto an arriving fisherman. Outside the sun promised another scorching day.

The six-cylinder Volvo fired at the first touch of the starter button. Tania coiled up the mooring ropes as Cliff took the boat astern; then, giving her full helm, he eased her forwards and out of the harbour. A white dory passed them and Tania gave the occupant a wave. He waved in return. She felt happy that day and it was contagious — Cliff actually whistled a few bars of 'The Dark Island'.

"See the huge bag of goodies Morag has given us!" Tania exclaimed. "We certainly won't die of starvation. In this part of the world they seem to think that missing a meal is nothing short of a catastrophe."

The launch was a 28-footer, clinker built, with the engine mounted amidships in the open well. Round the perimeter of the well was a continuous slatted bench. The forward cabin contained a couple more benches and a small table on which stood the gas cooker Captain Craig had promised. It was a trim little boat, Dempster thought, as it arrowed through the flat sea with the minimum of fuss. It would have been hard to have picked a better day.

The mainland peaks came into view as they moved away from the coast. Peaks with magical names: An Teallach rose before them — like a crown uplifted high, and the dark rocky coastline melted into the soothing calm of the sea. In the north-west, a tanker, long and low like a black log, was heading back from the Thule field. Tania lay back across the transom, her pale hair billowing out over the water and almost touching it. They were doing ten knots. A great spider's web of steel came into view, dwarfing the small cottages scattered along the shore at Strathcon, the village a few miles to the south of Inverloch.

"There it is." Tania sat up in the stern and pointed. "Consolidated Oil's new platform."

"Where you're taking me tomorrow?"

"The day after. It's part and parcel of the normal itinerary, if you were what you're supposed to be."

"I'd like to see it anyway. Looks interesting."

"It looks hideous," Tania retorted, shading her eyes as she lay back. "It looks like a monumental junk yard."

"You earn your living from the stuff. If you don't like it you shouldn't work for an oil company."

"Well, don't you think things will get spoiled, Cliff?" She gazed earnestly at him, but was only rewarded by a view of his broad back as he stared ahead once more.

"Yes, I do," he said eventually, "but I only work part-time for the oil moguls."

"Just think though — your brief may be to find out what Wilson's doing, but it could end up with a refinery at Rhuda."

"It certainly could if I don't succeed in getting to the bottom of the Wilson business." The rattle of industry from the platform reached them, effortlessly spanning the three miles which lay between. "He's doing his damnedest to get James to persuade his old man to sell it to some other outfit, but he may have to twist McBride's arm a bit harder — junkies aren't exactly dynamic."

James McBride rose unusually early that morning; normally he didn't stir before nine am He had been unable to sleep at all, and had grown tired of lying in bed. He went down the stairs, muttering discontentedly, and feeling a desperate need for narcotic sustenance. Caren was in the hall, preparing to go out.

"Going out with the Big Fisherman, Caren?" he mocked.

She flushed instantly, but retorted deliberately, "I noticed that you seemed to relish the lobster I brought back last time."

"Oh, I'm not complaining; bring some more if you can. I remember Alasdair MacAlasdair now. Thickset fellow with hands like canoe paddles. That's the one, isn't it? He was a well-known Grand Prix driver until he had a prang. Good going for a local man."

"Grand Prix?" Caren echoed.

"Yes — didn't he tell you? He's only a lobster fisherman by inclination. He owns several garages now, and a factory which makes car components or something."

"No," Caren answered slowly. "I knew he only fished for fun, but I hadn't realised that he was a racing driver — you say he had a crash?"

"Spectacular. It was a fantastic bit of news film. Anyway, that finished him."

Caren left James leaning against the granite lintel which spanned the hall fireplace like a miniature Stonehenge. Agnes had already lit the fire, but it gave out little heat as yet. It usually took about six hours for the mass of stone to warm up.

As she hurried eagerly down to the jetty, Caren thought she had never seen anyone who looked less 'finished' than Alasdair MacAlasdair.

Trigger MacKay, who had been keeping a strict eye on the road, went promptly to the telephoone in his office to report that a particular vehicle had left Inverloch.

"There are worse ways to earn a crust, Archie," the driver of the patrol car spoke wearily, for it was hot in the car and he couldn't be bothered to get out. "This is better than the trawlers, I can tell you — "

"Och, but look at the money you made, a wee fortune."

"Aye and just about killed myself in the process. You're not a sailor on the bloody boats — you're a zombie!" Ken, the driver, replied heatedly. "A bloody zombie. Four on, four off, night and day, and that's not counting for ripped nets and storms when you might have to work all round the clock."

"Well, I was ghillie-ing," returned Archie. "I suppose it might be better, but I didna think so. I'd rather be pounding the beat, like we used to do, any day of the week, than deal with city slicker stalkers; legs like goalposts sticking out of their kilts. It's wet nurses they're needing."

"When is this bloody car supposed to be coming past here, then?"

"Who can tell. Perhaps it'll stop first. Or turn down to Buitarkle — "

"Good. Then it's up to Stumper Carmichael to get his bloodshot eyes in focus."

"We'll maybe give it an hour. There's no great hurry, now, is there?"

"No, no. As long as I get back for a bite of lunch, I don't mind."

PC Archibald Duncan stifled another yawn. They were parked just off the main road into Ullapool, where the Inverloch and Buitarkle road joined it. In the latter village the generally quick eyes of PC Carmichael were closed: he was enjoying forty winks before lunch.

The patrol car was well screened by flowering whin bushes, so only part of the windscreen was visible from the main road.

"There's a car coming along the Inverloch road now," remarked Archie. "I caught a glimpse of it on the rise." His companion took his hat off, slid out of the car, and peered through the bushes. As the vehicle came up to the main road junction, Archie picked up the mike from the facia, and gave his call sign.

"Archie here, Willie. That bloody car went past about a minute ago... Roger, Archie."

"Better watch your procedure," Ken warned. "The Super was on about it. Said it was becoming like the fishermen's wave band!"

"That must be the island over there, on the left," Tania pointed. "What's its name again?"

"Gruinard."

"Gives me the willies. How about some coffee?"

"Good idea," Cliff grunted, putting on sunglasses against the fierce glare off the sea.

Tania moved forward from her stern seat and placed the plastic carrier on the deck at Cliff's feet.

"Seems to be a smell of gas in the cabin, Cliff." She unscrewed the flask tops and measured coffee carefully.

"Hmm. I noticed it too. If you'll take the wheel, I'll have a look when I've had my coffee."

"Your coffee, sir," she held the cup out to him. "Is that the topmast of the *Celtic Pioneer* down there?" she asked, looking out to starboard.

"It could be," he decided. He placed the coffee on a ledge in front of him and picked up his binoculars. "Yes, that's definitely her. She's further out than I thought," he altered course slightly. It was exactly 11.45 am when a shattering explosion blew the front of the boat apart.

10

DEMPSTER WAS THROWN up in the air and Tania was hurled backwards, stunned by the cabin door. It took rather less than two minutes for the bows to sink, forcing the stern up out of the sea, like the tail of a drake diving amongst reeds.

The cold water revived Cliff. He spat out a mouthful of it, shook his head and looked about him. Tania was floating face upwards on the other side of the wrecked boat. She was unconscious. He swam over, grabbed her by the hair, and towed her towards the stern, clambering aboard and hauling her onto his wet perch. He hoped the stern was going to stay afloat. Half the buoyancy tanks under the seat round the gunwales had been ripped out by the explosion, but the rear of the boat had settled, so that its rectangular stern was practically horizontal.

Water streamed off both of them and Tania's breathing against his shoulder was erratic. Laying her carefully down on the precarious surface, he ripped open her blouse and unfastened her bra, then applying his mouth to hers forced air slowly and rhythmically into her lungs. Gradually her respiration improved and she opened large puzzled green eyes.

"Cliff?"

"How are you feeling?"

"What...what happened?"

"We went bang." He gestured at the debris bobbing in the water around them. Tania tried to raise herself on an elbow, but gave up and sank back again.

"Are you hurt?" He gazed at her anxiously.

"No, just a bit sore and battered, and my throat feels awful."

"That's from swallowing salt water. Try and lie still. The sun will soon warm you. I should take off the rest of your clothes, otherwise you'll get cold again." He grinned as Tania noticed her torn blouse for the first time.

"I had to start undressing you in order to get you back in working order. But I expect you can finish the job yourself. Don't mind me. I'll just watch."

"All right," she smiled weakly, "I do feel cold." She unzipped her jeans and started to ease them off. Cliff pulled them gently from her ankles. There were some large ugly bruises down her left side. "I must have lost my sandals," she remarked, looking confusedly at her bare feet.

"Don't worry." Cliff found himself reflecting abstractedly on how people involved in serious accidents often lost their boots and shoes. He remembered seeing a man hit by a car whose boots remained exactly where he had been standing, in the middle of the road, while he was impaled against a wall thirty feet away. Wriggling out of his own damp trousers, his mind was brought back to the immediate present with a jolt, as he detected the drift of the wreck. His jaw tightened, but he said nothing.

"Was it that gas that exploded?" Tania asked, watching him rub his brown legs vigorously with his hands. "But we weren't even using it, were we?"

"Could have been a short circuit in the lighting wire in the cabin, as the battery's in the engine box. Was, rather."

"But that smell of gas was ominous."

"By rights it shouldn't be allowed on boats." He straightened up, combing his thick black hair out of his eyes with his fingers.

Tania turned to gaze towards the land where the dark shoreline was sandwiched between the red sandstone and gneiss cliffs and the green sea below. "What next?" she asked quietly. "Any good shouting for help?"

"Too far from the shore." He gazed at the rocky headland beyond the island.

"I always fancied being marooned on a desert island, but this isn't quite so funny, is it?"

78

"No, there are islands and islands and that one ahead is deserted for a very good reason."

High above the crags of Gruinard Bay, a figure stood looking out to sea. He held a pair of 10 x 50 Zeiss binoculars in his hands. His face wore a peculiarly satisfied expression. He had heard the dull explosion, like the deep whoomph of a quarry blast, and his Bulova Accutron told him that it had occurred within a minute of the scheduled time.

Tania was worried. She wondered what on earth was going to happen, but completely lacked the strength to do anything to save herself. If they were swept out to sea there wasn't any land until Canada or Greenland, unless they bumped into Iceland first. She stared bleakly at the landward skyline. She noticed it had moved.

"Cliff, I think we're drifting. I've watched two rocks on the hill over there." She pointed to the land rising above the island. "They were in line a minute ago, and they aren't any longer," she said simply.

"I'm afraid you're right," he admitted. They were drifting quite rapidly towards anthrax island. "This current's fairly powerful. It must be all of four knots. Do you swim, Tania?" He looked at her, weighing up her physical and mental reserves.

"Used to do quite a lot. Too many other activities take up my spare time these days."

"Such as?"

"Oh — boyfriends, lots of them." She laughed weakly, her eyes held a glimmer of the old sparkle. "And then I have to spend time keeping my judo up to scratch in order to control them."

"Well, you may yet have a chance to show me your racing crawl." Grimly he added, "It would happen just at this point with the tide coming in."

A section of cabin door frame had floated in with them. The door had been ripped from the hinges, leaving a U-shape of three inch by two inch framing with bits of jagged hardboard cabin lining still tacked onto it, like fragments of brown paper.

Also attached was a short length of black flex and behind a section of hardboard something else, a small cylindrical object, the size of a thimble which Cliff found difficulty in identifying. Laboriously he pulled the debris towards him, using another piece of floating wood as a boat hook.

"What is it?"

Leaning well out and holding onto the stem of the rudder with one hand, he dragged the frame aboard. The binding tape had lost most of its adhesive qualities in the water, but still held the small black cylinder in place. Before the explosion, he realised, it would have been concealed from sight on the top of the door frame.

Tania's voice was very quiet. "Cliff, was that explosion deliberate?"

He looked up sharply from his examination. "Looks like it. Dirty work at the crossroads." Ridiculously, he heard himself keeping his voice light so as not to alarm the girl. But she didn't seem to be the type who was going to throw a fit of hysterics. Instead Tania held out her hand for the now dismantled cylinder.

"It's a miniature time switch," he said, putting on his now nearly dry trousers. "Cunning Nippons."

"A time switch?" She set it on her brown shapely knees to examine the mechanism. "Oh, like the thing on the immerser in my flat."

"Same sort of idea, only considerably smaller, and designed for immersing us."

"But how?"

"Triggered to a switch which activated when I started the engine, or possibly when we got into the boat, and wired via the cabin lighting circuit to a simple ignition fuse. A small hole in the gas supply pipe," he glanced at his watch, "two hours' accumulation of gas, and we should have been reduced to the contents of the ex-carrier bag. I bet the knob would have been taken off the gas cylinder, too, so that we couldn't turn it off. And it was precisely timed so that we would be close to this desirable island when it blew up. Someone must have studied the tides and known the cruising speed of the launch."

"But who would want to do a... How many people knew we were coming here?"

"Oh, everyone knew that. It's great how word travels in these Highland villages."

"It's quite horrible to think of," Tania said in a small voice. "It's the first time anyone has shown so much interest in my welfare for a long time."

"Oh, I've been keeping an eye on you," Dempster spoke softly.

"Have you, Cliff?"

"What would Swartze say if he knew I'd asked his secretary if she'd make love on the wreck of a company launch?"

"He'd know better than to interfere. His secretary can make her own decisions, but I'm sure she could think of a better time and place... "

"That, Miss Olsen, seems as good a reason for moving on from here as any of the other reasons. And one of the other reasons is getting awfully pressing."

Gruinard Island was now barely a hundred yards away — an inviting haven set in an emerald sea, but they could already see the regularly spaced white squares which were the warning boards.

"What on earth are we to do? Swim?"

"We'll have to eventually," Cliff told her gently. "If we aim for the north side of the island there's a chance the tide will carry us into Little Loch Broom. Do you think you can make it?" He watched her out of dark, brooding eyes.

"I can try... Not much alternative is there?"

"No," he replied slowly. "No, there isn't, but if we get round the tip of the island, we might be spotted by someone on shore."

"How far is the shore?"

"About three quarters of a mile, I would guess."

Dempster carefully stowed the thimble-like time switch in a pocket of his jeans.

"Someone," said Tania, watching him, "has a very warped sense of humour."

Two eider ducks rose close by them, their wings beating the air industriously in take off. Far out to sea, the mast of another

81

giant tanker was just visible, its 200,000-ton hull deep with ballast.

PC Jamie MacCormack's beat extended officially from the Corrieshallach Gorge to a western margin on the coast itself, running south via a tortuous route, a tattered array of islands and headlands as far as Loch Ewe. Jamie was in two minds as to how to take the day. He wasn't issued with an official police car so he used his own, a well-worn Austin, tired and asthmatic, the latter complaint stemming from a loose carburettor manifold which had been slack for the past five years. It was in this less than trusty steed that he had taken the westerly road from his neat little pre-cast concrete block bungalow at 10.10 am that morning. It was sunny and warm and he had anticipated a good day out. He called in at the Bellows Bar of the Forge Hotel and bought two cans of McEwan's Export and two packets of crisps from the owner, Donald Jamieson. It was that sort of day... He also took an old pair of field glasses which he himself had found on the beach at Durness, when he'd been on holiday two years ago, and which hadn't been claimed.

PC Willie Watson from Ullapool had phoned him an hour earlier, telling him to keep his eyes open for a certain car, which might come his way. On the other hand, it might just as easily take the Garve and Dingwall road from Braemore junction at the Corrieshallach Gorge. Unobtrusive observation was what Willie had demanded from his plain clothes colleague. So Jamie drove dutifully along the narrow road past the crofts, wondering if he had time to go in and see Alex Campbell, who also played in the Dundonnell shinty team, when a horn sounded discreetly behind him. Displaying the good manners of one who is not in any particular hurry, he waved the other car past.

"Well, well," he said to himself. "If it isn't the man in question!" The driver of the other car pipped his horn again in acknowledgment as he swept by. It was eight miles further on that he found the same car parked in a layby, close to the gneiss outcrops of Gruinard Bay; there was no sign of its owner. Jamie continued on, unperturbed, and drew into an old quarry close to the Gruinard river.

A can of beer stowed in each pocket, his binoculars slung round his neck, he made his way along the river bank, then slanted off up the hill. Perspiring, he removed his tweed jacket and carried it over his arm. His intention was to follow a small fast-flowing burn up to the crest of the shoulder, which rose above the rock outcrops and extended to the high hill country to the west of An Teallach.

At that precise moment, the explosion occurred, but Jamie was busy crossing the burn at the time, and failed to hear it. He gained the ridge at about the 900-foot contour and settled himself comfortably, his back against a boulder. The terrain below him was mainly heather and rock, with clusters of silver birch. The coastline spread like an unfinished jigsaw puzzle. The sun blazed down with an unusual intensity; islands sparkled like jewels randomly scattered over the sea — the Summer Isles, Priest's Island, Eilean Dubh. Names fit for a fairy tale land...

Jamie removed his glasses from distant shores and islands and returned to the job in hand.

"Now where has that bugger got to?" he asked himself. He studied the rocky ground below and soon picked up the bright blue of a pullover. "Ah," his tone was one of satisfaction, and he reached into his pocket for a can of beer. "Now I can get to work." He opened the can deftly and, still holding the glasses to his eyes, took a sip of beer. The man below appeared in partial silhouette against the shoots of young bracken; he was gazing out to sea, through binoculars. Now Jamie had an unfortunate habit of jumping to hasty conclusions, so he instantly assumed that the giant tanker, easily visible from their elevated station, was the object of the man's interest. He thought he would be smart and give Jack Gillies, the coastguard down at Rudhe Reidh, a ring: he would know the boat. That would look good in his report... He accomplished the almost impossible feat of sniffing as he finished his drink. It was shortly after the tanker had vanished beneath the horizon that the other man stood up and started back down the hill. Jamie followed at a discreet distance, making ample use of the cover provided by the terrain.

11

PC Jamie MacCormack's friend, Alex Campbell, was a crofter, but he also possessed a few lobster creels. He sold his catch to Donald Jamieson, owner of the Forge Hotel. In a good week the profit covered his drinking money, provided he was abstemious.

At two pm that afternoon, Alex was cutting along Little Loch Broom as fast as his tinny outboard would permit on his way back from lifting his catch. He was whistling 'The Hen's March to the Midden', one of his favourite airs. He had plenty to be happy about: the lobsters had been good that week and his cattle subsidy had just come through. To his right the hillside rose above the road, gneiss-topped on the higher slopes, culminating in the bare flesh of Torridonian sandstone on the summit of An Teallach. What he saw to his left stopped him in mid whistle. With a Gaelic oath he turned the boat hastily twenty degrees to starboard and closed on the objects he had caught sight of in the water. Two people. There was a girl, her head held clear of the water by a man.

Alex cut the engine and drifted alongside them. "I'll take her." He wasted no time in speech, but simply reached down and caught the girl by the armpits, lifting her on board with the water streaming off her. She gave a moan and hung limp in his arms, like a sack of corn, as he laid her gently in the bottom of the boat, her head resting on the forward transom. He kicked aside three lobsters. Dempster pulled himself laboriously aboard, rocking the boat dangerously, and gasped his thanks as he collapsed onto a net beside Tania. Alex Campbell deftly retrieved the lobsters in the well of the boat and threw them into a bucket. Then he took off his jacket and pullover and draped them over the girl.

"You warm enough?" he enquired briefly.

"I'm all right just now. She's suffering from exposure."

Alex asked no more questions, but revved the engine and swept up the loch, as Cliff started to shiver uncontrollably. Twelve minutes later they had moored and their rescuer was carrying Tania through the door of his cottage, which stood down between the sea loch and the road. He laid her carefully on the sofa, turned on two bars of an electric fire and stirred up the coal fire already banked in the hearth. Dempster closed the door behind him. He looked pale beneath his tan.

"How is she?"

"Oh, she'll do fine. Better dry yourself." Alex offered Cliff a towel, as Tania's eyelids flickered open.

"You're all right now, lassie. Safe and sound. Just you lie still," the crofter assured her, vanishing through the door into the next room.

"I'll dry you," Cliff offered. Though the heat from the two fires warmed the room, they were both shivering. Gently he rubbed her feet. Alex returned with an armful of logs, and surveyed his visitors assessingly. It was a hard man for sure, and built like a stirk, but near to exhaustion now. Firmly he thrust another towel into Cliff's hands. "You'd better use this for yourself now, and then relax for a bit. It'll do ye a power o' good."

"Thanks," Cliff said. "For everything. My name is Hugh Spencer, by the way and this is Tania Olsen."

"Alex Campbell. Pleased to meet you both," returned the other as gravely as if they had just been introduced in the High Street of Inverness. "Will I call Dr Moncrieff? He's only a few miles up the road and there's a call box not a hundred yards away."

Cliff remembered assuring their rescuer that there was no need. He remembered sinking back into an old deep armchair, and relaxing his tense body, and the next thing he was aware of

85

was Tania standing looking down at him with a tea cup in her hand, dressed in funereal black of fifty years ago.

"Feeling better?" she asked softly, taking the towel from his knees.

"All right, now, I guess. But when I opened my eyes I had a horrible feeling we were both attending your funeral."

"The dress used to be my mother's," Alex commented from the doorway. "It's been lying in a drawer for ten years, but there now, there's a use for everything after all. Now here's a cup of tea and dry clothes for you Mr Spencer. You must get out of those wet things. My, they're fair steaming." He handed Cliff an old pair of plus fours, heavy Harris wool stockings, a shirt and a seaman's pullover. "They'll no be a vera good fit, you know," he added dubiously, "but it's all I've got."

As Cliff emerged from the bathroom he heard Tania explaining with disarmingly feminine vagueness how their boat just blew up, and Alex was waxing eloquent on the subject of Gruinard Island.

"It used to give good grazing, so it did, in my father's time, and look at it now — cherms, cherms, until the next century. Unless they provide the money to clean it up."

"Could they decontaminate it, then?" Tania asked.

"Och, yes. I've run the scientists out there myself. They could indeed. But it would cost a lot of money. If that island were in the south of England, now..." he paused eloquently.

Emile Casini spent a pleasant afternoon fishing from the hotel boat. He rowed out towards the harbour entrance and was fortunate enough to catch twenty rock cod which he carried up to the hotel in two plastic buckets, his fishing rod slipping from under his arm.

McCallum came to meet him at the front door.

"Ah, let me give you a hand, Mr Casini." Deftly he removed the rod case, and relieved his guest of one of the buckets, doing rapid mental arithmetic as he surveyed the contents. "Well, well, that's a bonnie pickle of fish you have. I never thought you'd get anything."

"A lucky day, Mr McCallum." Casini's smile extended like an elastic band. "Are these any good to you?"

"Certainly, certainly." It represented a helpful economy. "I think you have more talent than many of our guests, Mr Casini."

"But salt water fish does not really count, I believe. It's the salmon. That's what I'm after."

"Patience, Mr Casini, patience."

Caren McBride was in Inverloch that day. She had dropped Agnes on her afternoon off, and as it was such a sunny afternoon she had decided to take a walk along the sea front before returning home. She was dawdling by the sea wall, watching a seine netter coming into harbour, when a voice behind her said, "It's a long time since I last saw you."

Caren whirled round, laughing, for she knew the voice. It struck a chord in her heart that she hadn't known existed.

"Yes, Alasdair," she agreed demurely. "It must be all of six hours!"

"I didn't know you frequented this backwater."

"Oh yes, I'm just Annabel Lee in the mornings."

"Come on into the cottage then, and have a cup of tea. I make it myself."

"Aren't you clever?" she teased. "I thought you lived on raw lobster and fresh air."

Alasdair MacAlasdair, Caren had to admit, was a good housewife. His cottage was snug and orderly. The only vaguely uncomfortable object in sight was an underwater gun, propped in the corner of the living room. She thought of Alasdair's friend who had died and shuddered briefly.

"Yes," he said, reading her thoughts, "that's John's."

"It looks a vicious bit of work. Poor fish."

"Poor John."

Caren turned to the mantelpiece. "I love those," she said, admiring the china dogs which stood either end.

"Wallie dugs." Alasdair smiled. "Yes, I've left everything just as my people had it. It's peaceful isn't it?"

At that moment the telephone chose to ring. Alasdair

grimaced. "Blast the thing. It was my one mistake to have that installed."

"Never mind, Alasdair. I'll go and make the tea for you"

"Right. Help yourself. The things are in the back kitchen, through there… Inverloch 251?"

There was a noise of money being fed into a public call box and then a familiar voice: "Hello, Alasdair? Cliff here. Can you come down to Dundonnell right away and pick us up? I borrowed a launch from the *Celtic Pioneer* and it's blown up."

"You all right?"

"Just a bit cold. But could be somebody wanted me out of the way."

"I'll come now."

"Just a moment. Can you collect some clothes from the hotel for me and for Tania Olsen?"

"Tania Olsen?"

"Er, yes. Did I not mention her? My cover, on loan from Swartze."

"Well, well."

"I'm wearing a crofter's plus fours and Tania's dressed for a funeral."

"Not yours, I hope."

"I'll survive."

"Won't it blow your cover if I go for your clothes — Mr Spencer?"

"Oh just tell Morag something vague about knowing me years ago and meeting up by chance. And mention we had a small accident with the launch."

"I'll do that."

"Thanks, Alasdair, and would you send a message to the *Celtic Pioneer* via the coastguard? Captain Craig will be wondering where the hell we've got to."

"Surely. Now where will I find you in Dundonnell?"

Willing as Alasdair was to rush to the aid of a friend in need, he saw no good reason why the activity should deprive him of Caren's continued company, and for her part she was more than content to join the relief operation which began with the organising of a goggle-eyed Morag in quest of clothing at the

Stob Dearg. Alasdair's friend, Caren soon realised, was the man from the oil company who had visited Rhuda the previous day.

"He's the tall, dark and silent type, right," she said. "A bit on the formidable side."

"That's him." Alasdair grinned.

"And I liked Tania. She's rather striking too, a real Nordic blonde, you know. She was awfully nice."

Her companion's grin broadened as he reversed out of the hotel fore-court muttering about dark horses being led to the water, and it served them right when they fell in it.

The Jaguar, which Alasdair drove with considerable style, ate up the mileage. Its possession was an aspect of Alasdair MacAlasdair which reminded Caren of her brother James's thumbnail sketch, and the need to revise her first opinions of the simple lobsterman who had picked her up off the jetty at Rhuda. That had only been a few short days ago, but it seemed in a funny way as if she had known him for years.

At Dundonnell introductions were made, the crofter's plus fours were returned to their owner, along with the black dress, and Alex Campbell's offer of a wee dram from a fine bottle he had by him for just such occasions was regretfully declined.

"Well, why do you think someone tried to blow you to bits?" Alasdair asked, as he took a corner at speed, the large car filling up most of the road. He caught Cliff's quick look in the driving mirror to see if the girls had heard the remark in the back. "You can trust Caren to be discreet," he said simply.

"Of course, Hugh." She leaned forward. "Even if you're about to confess to scuttling the oil company launch yourself."

Cliff turned in his seat. "Then promise you'll keep this conversation to yourself, Caren, because in a way what's going on is indirectly connected with Rhuda." The smile vanished from her face. "Don't be alarmed. But you know, do you, your father has had an offer or two for the estate — "

"Which he's refused. The subject's not very popular at home. He even had some awful high-powered tycoon character from one oil company flying in to see him personally."

89

"My boss," Tania smiled at this view of Mr Swartze. "Don't forget I work for Consolidated Oil."

"And I'm really up here to look into security arrangements for them," explained Cliff. "Hugh Spencer is a cover. I'm afraid I'm no relation to your father's old friend, Sir Hubert, at all. My real name is Dempster, Cliff Dempster. I tell you this, Caren, because the sale of Rhuda estate seems to be in the middle of things and maybe you can help by keeping your eyes and ears open." He could hardly spell out that he wanted her to spy on her own brother. "You could let Alasdair here know if anything unusual crops up."

"Have you known about this all along, Alasdair?" Caren asked.

"I'm not involved in the oil security Cliff is here to sort out, but there's been a very under-explained death in Inverloch recently — "

"Your friend?"

"And Cliff's, too as it happens. If there's any connection between that and what Cliff is looking into for Consolidated Oil, then we're both in it, all the way." Alasdair glared fiercely ahead at the road for a moment. "What we need is something in the way of evidence, instead of speculation."

"How would you rate a time switch, then, similar to those used in the more sophisticated timebombs?" Cliff asked, and produced his trophy.

"And that blew up your boat?" Caren interjected.

"Probably triggered to set a detonator off a certain number of hours after the engine was started, that and a leaking propane gas cylinder in the cabin to provide the woomf. What d'you think, Alasdair?"

"That would probably do the trick, all right," his friend admitted. "Okay how, but any idea who and why?"

"I can't believe that somebody deliberately tried to kill us," Tania said quietly.

"I don't know if it was necessarily intended to kill us, but it was certainly meant to put me out of circulation for some time."

"Which means someone else, beside us, knows you're not Hugh Spencer. How d'you manage to get your cover blown so fast, friend?" There was a hint of the old professional mockery in Alasdair's voice.

"There was that man out at the Centre who'd worked for UK Lubricants," pointed out Tania. "But he seemed totally harmless."

"No," Dempster said, "if it was anybody we've met, my money's on that pilot, Jack Bourne, the one who flew us up from London. He recognised me all right. It's just bad luck he knew somebody it would be worth his while telling."

"And who might that somebody be?"

"Paul Wilson?" offered Tania.

"I think," Cliff squinted thoughtfully at the small piece of electronic gadgetry in his lap, "we might keep a closer watch on Emile Casini."

"That's one of the rival oilmen staying at the hotel," Tania explained to Caren.

"After all, he's the only one who's been buzzing around us asking friendly questions ever since we arrived."

Alasdair laughed. "You know, up until half an hour ago I'd have had your Sicilian friend down on my suspect list too. But since meeting the other half of your cover story, Cliff, I am forced to entertain the possibility that the man's only human, and it's not you he is interested in at all."

Tania chuckled. "I'll let you all know, if I find out the answer to that one. Like Alasdair, I feel sure Emile's motives are — how should I put it — more down to earth." She liked Alasdair. There was something solidly dependable about him. And in his company Cliff's guard seemed to come down and leave him relaxed and approachable. Beside her on the back seat, Caren began to talk about Gruinard Island and anthrax. After listening to Alex Campbell's views on the subject at some length while Cliff had been out phoning, Tania had no difficulty in matching the other girl's indignation.

In the front Alasdair said, "Talking of Casini, Cliff, I've been having a wee chat with Trigger MacKay. Casini was at the Point House the day Trigger went round to do his check up on boats' comings and goings the night John died."

"Did he speak to him?"

91

"No, no. Apparently, Trigger just saw him through a window."

"Interesting."

"Didn't you say that Anglo-Italian had bought that place?" Tania asked. "That's right," answered Alasdair.

"That's the company that annoyed Dad so much to begin with," Caren chimed in. "Before your boss came up, Tania," she explained. "They turned him right off the whole idea. He showed me one of their letters. They were most presumptuous, but then they did offer an awful lot of money."

"Huh, Anglo-Italian haven't got a very good reputation in the trade," Tania put in.

"Not surprised if they employ those dudes up at the Point House. Anything more on them, Alasdair?" Cliff asked.

"Not much yet, I'm afraid. But I saw the character John recognised when I was going to my creels yesterday morning. He's called Bernadino. A really big guy. You couldn't mistake him."

"John was definite about his background, was he?"

"Sure. Said it gave him quite a shock to see that villain walking round a quiet little backwater like Inverloch. The other chap, the agent or whatever he is, goes by the name of Stewart. I think I saw him around in a cream Volks and took him to be a tourist. Dark bloke with a moustache and a floozie in attendance. Possibly his wife. He's supposed to be married. She comes down to Dochy's for bread and milk. Nice looking, dresses flashy."

"What's the place being used for?"

"I think it's going to be a sort of admin for their platform operation. Not enough room there for anything else. The water's not deep enough. Only four fathoms round the spit. They've a good boat," he added. "A pilot cutter, one of those twin diesel jobs that can knock up about thirty knots if pressed."

"What size?"

"Thirty-five footer, I'd say. Nice lines. Wouldn't mind her myself."

"Do you think it might have run down A.J.?"

"No. It was probably a plastic screw that did that."

Alasdair slowed down as they came into Inverloch, and as he dropped Cliff and Tania off at the hotel, Dempster paused.

"I think you and I should pay the Point House a quiet visit quite soon, Alasdair."

"Okay by me."

"Tonight?"

"Why not?"

Thanks to Morag, word of their misadventure had already spread well round the guests and staff of the Stob Dearg hotel, and there was a reception committee avid for all the details. McCallum himself emerged from the kitchen quarters, a mound of rock cod freshly gutted for dinner, glistening wetly in the bowl he had been inspecting when his guests arrived.

"That's a fine catch you've got there," observed Cliff who had got tired of repeating the edited version of the afternoon's accident.

"Mr Casini's work."

"He must have had a busy day."

"Oh, it didn't take him long. He knows what he's about, that one. Just a few hours in the dinghy."

As he was retreating upstairs behind Tania, Cliff heard a voice below at Reception which he thought he recognised. On an impulse he retraced his steps to a point where he could look down into the foyer. James McBride was leaning on the counter speaking with Morag. Whatever was said was brief, for he left almost immediately.

Alasdair drove Caren to where her car was parked at the end of the street in Inverloch. They hadn't spoken since they dropped Cliff and Tania. As she opened the door she said, "They're trying to force Dad to sell Rhuda, aren't they, Alasdair?" Her eyes were sad.

"Not Cliff. He's only hired to do a job. But there *is* some dirty work going on, whatever the police think."

"Do you think John Pollock died because he found out something?" she asked quietly.

"Yes, I do, and Cliff and I are going to find out what it was.

Caren, I promise I'll tell you if anything at all comes up that could affect your father or the estate." They stood together beside her car.

"One other thing, Alasdair."

"Hmm?"

"You'll…you'll take care, when you and Cliff…you know…"

"Oh course." He smiled affectionately at her. "After all, I've got a date first thing in the morning that nobody's going to make me miss." As he bent to close the car door for her, she kissed him lightly on the lips.

"I'll be there," she said.

Alasdair's neighbours, Mr and Mrs Todd, had been drawing the old age pension for the past twenty years and intended to continue indefinitely. As they saw him go in next door they complained to each other about the lobster which Alasdair had thoughtfully presented to them that morning. Shell fish are seldom popular with the older folk of the Scottish seaboard.

"I'd rather have a good bit of saithe any day," grumbled Mr Todd to his wife, and she was equally disparaging.

"Too many people get that pantomime poisoning with these things."

Next door Alasdair dreamed of Caren as he sat down to his plate of saithe, content in the knowledge that at least two old people were having a good meal that night, though he would have preferred lobster himself.

12

AT 6.20 PM the white hull of the *Celtic Pioneer* appeared at the entrance to Inverloch harbour. Captain Craig sounded a short warning blast on the siren for the benefit of several small craft scuttling about. These apart, the harbour was relatively empty. The fishing vessels had put out to sea earlier that morning on their way to fishing grounds in the North Minch. They had each received a visit from Trigger MacKay before they left. Several truckloads of supplies for the *Celtic Pioneer* were waiting on the pier. The Captain signalled half astern and a slight tremor shook the thousand-ton ship. Water bubbled round her propellers.

Dempster watched her draw close to the pier, then went down the passage to knock at Tania's door.

"Who's there?"

"It's me. Cliff."

"Come in." She was standing by the wash basin, drying her hair with a towel. "Excuse the informality," she laughed, "but I really wasn't receiving visitors. I'm repairing the damage, and next I'm going to soak in a lovely hot bath for at least an hour."

"Mind you don't drown."

She turned in a flash, threw the towel at his face, and had a wrist lock on his right arm before he could dodge. Instinctively he rolled backwards with her across the bed, twisting and landing his full weight on top of her, effectively breaking the lock.

"Well," she gasped as he eased back and looked down at her. "Mr Swartze *will* be pleased to know your reflexes are still functioning."

"You ought to be convalescing, Miss Olsen," he answered with mock severity. "I really think I had better stay and make sure you do what you're told."

"It's certainly a more suitable time and place than this afternoon," she agreed meekly, as Dempster rose and locked the door.

Some time later Mr McCallum's receptionist saw Cliff Dempster walking purposefully through the hall.

"You back for dinner, Mr Spencer?" she called.

"Yes, Morag. I'm just going over to the *Celtic Pioneer* to tell Captain Craig we're all right — and commiserate about his boat."

"You were certainly very lucky."

"We sure were."

"If you're going down the pier, the mail for the boat is here, do you want to take it over?"

"Sure."

She turned to one of the cubbyholes behind the desk and handed him a bundle held together with an elastic band.

Dempster glanced at the package as he went out. On top was an unstamped envelope with a crest of an eagle surrounded by a holly wreath in the upper left corner. It was addressed to 'Paul Wilson, *Celtic Pioneer*'. He remembered where he had seen that crest before. Above the entrance to Rhuda House the stone was so weathered that at the time he had trouble in making out what it represented. Fortunately the envelope was not very well sealed and he was able to ease the flap deftly open with a nailfile. Rapidly he scanned the single sheet.

Paul,
As I have to come into Inverloch today, I thought I would leave this note for you. I can see you tonight at the Western Atlantic for dinner, at say 8.15? If you can't manage give a ring. By the way, a chap called Hugh Spencer, from UK Lubricants, was here yesterday and mentioned your name, which made me wonder. Not much development on the home front yet. Believe me, these things take time.
Yours,
James

Cliff ran his tongue round the envelope flap and replaced the envelope in the pile. On the gangplank of the *Celtic Pioneer* he met the ship's engineer and handed the bundle of letters over to him.

The Captain was busy writing in his cabin when Dempster knocked at the door. He was wearing glasses and looked much older.

"Well, well, Hugh. Good to see you alive. I hope my Tania is still in one piece?"

"She's fine, and sends her apologies. She's having a bath right now. Er, I'm sorry about the launch."

"To hell with the launch, as long as you two survived. I suppose you've had enough people telling you how lucky you've been. We went up past Gruinard on our way back, but saw no sign of the wreck."

"Probably sunk by then, I imagine. We abandoned ship just off the island."

"What d'you think happened?"

Once more Cliff recited the edited version of the explosion.

"I don't understand it." Craig shook his head. "That boat was well maintained. I've had a word with Sparks about it, but he's like an old woman with the electrics. He checks everything." Frowning, the Captain began filling his pipe with Condor Sliced. There was a knock at the cabin door and Paul Wilson looked in.

"I'm just off — Oh, I didn't know you were here, Hugh. You okay?"

"Sure."

"Had a narrow escape, I hear."

"Guess we did." Craig explained what had happened. It was hard to believe Wilson had any previous knowledge of the accident. He seemed genuinely concerned. Either that or a bloody good actor, Dempster thought.

"We had a scout about at the entrance of Little Loch Broom on the way north, did the Captain tell you? But we didn't see anything. Not a single piece of flotsam."

"There's a strong current running into the loch," said the

Captain. "If the boat's not on the bottom by now, it's probably cast up close by the Forge Hotel."

Paul glanced at his watch. "Well, I've got to go. See you in the morning."

"Got a girl tucked away somewhere, Paul?" Captain Craig looked up, a twinkle in his eye, as he lit his pipe.

"No such luck," Paul was already at the door. "See you around, Hugh. We must fix up that climb. I've had an idea what we could try. Sorry I can't stop now. See you."

"How about you?" Cliff asked, after the scientist had left. "Are you having dinner with us tonight?"

"Ah, I don't think so, thanks, Hugh." Craig indicated the pile of papers on his desk. "I've got rather a lot of this bumf to plough through tonight. I'll grab a bite here in a minute."

"Well in that case I guess I'd better be leaving you to it." Cliff straightened up. Instead of returning to his work, the Captain gazed up at his guest speculatively through a cloud of smoke.

"Swartze told me I was to help you if I could."

"That was good of him."

"I gathered that he thought you were somebody special." The Captain's voice had dropped perceptibly. "I'm not one to pry," he continued, "but anything I can do to help — just let me know, will you? No questions asked."

"I won't forget, Captain. And thanks. It's good to know. Meanwhile, as I'm here, could I take myself on an unguided tour of the ship?"

"Go ahead. It's all yours."

"Thanks."

Dempster left the cabin and went on deck. He could see Wilson walking along the road past the Stob Dearg Hotel. Swartze's briefing dossier had held a plan of the *Celtic Pioneer* and he guessed Wilson's cabin would be one of the bigger ones situated aft. There was nobody else about. Noises and laughter below suggested the crew were eating. The second of the row of cabins aft bore the helpful label 'Wilson, P'. Less helpfully it was locked. Cliff took a short section of heat treated twelve-gauge wire from his pocket. A few minutes later the door swung open and he slipped inside.

It was a large and comfortable cabin. A hi-fi stereo cassette deck had been installed in a long wall cupboard; a bunk covered by a bright floral bedspread occupied the same side of the cabin. A table and two chairs, a wardrobe, and a settee made up the sum total of the furniture. Several photographic enlargements were fixed on the walls: climbing scenes. One was of high mountains, probably the Hindu Kush, thought Dempster. There were other peaks too, and shots of Wilson climbing in various parts of the world. Bit of a Narcissus, our Paul, I shouldn't wonder, decided Cliff. An enormous enlargement of El Capitan, the mountain on which Paul had been injured, occupied the far wall. He glanced in at a small bathroom adjoining the cabin — nothing there.

Cliff worked with speed and efficiency and it took him precisely five minutes to find the first item of interest — a map of Rhuda Estate. It had been Sellotaped in an amateur fashion to the underside of one of the drawers below the bunk, an OS 6″ Series 1, with the Rhuda march added in blue biro. Dempster replaced it. There were papers in the table drawers: bills, and a pile of newspaper cuttings, mostly about Wilson's work for the company. Nothing there. He glanced in the wardrobe and found, besides a good selection of clothes, a Nikon with several lenses, securely lodged behind a wooden shoe bar at the bottom of the wardrobe. He was about to close the wardrobe, then, curious, he picked up the leather case which contained a 135mm telephoto lens and took it out. He unscrewed the bayonet dust cap and peered inside. A piece of paper lay neatly inside the perimeter of the lens casing. He gave a low whistle of satisfaction and eased it out with a pencil. It was a newspaper cutting, dated March, two years previously.

HUNT FOR SOUTHAMPTON
POLICE ATTACKER

The Police would like to interview a man in connection with the assault of a police officer which took place during one of the largest drug hauls in recent years. The one and a half million pound consignment of hard drugs was discovered aboard the SS *Bahore* when it berthed at Southampton yesterday.

The discovery was made by a specially trained drug dog. 'Saint', when the vessel docked at two pm. The 18,000-ton ship, which was carrying chemicals from Karachi for Anglo-India Fertiliser, left Karachi twenty-two days ago.

During a search by the Drug Squad a man, not a member of the crew, assaulted and seriously injured twenty-three year old Detective Constable Jack Wooler with an iron bar. The constable, of 22 Moorland Road, Southampton, was admitted to the South Hants Hospital, and a hospital spokesman said his condition last night was still serious. Constable Wooler is married with an eight-week-old daughter.

The police have issued a description of the man they want to interview in connection with the assault as about 26 years of age, with a public school accent, slim built, about five foot ten, with a sallow complexion and brown hair. He was wearing a light gabardine overcoat and grey trousers.

Fazil Mohammed, described as a deckhand, is at present being detained for questioning.

Below the paragraphs was a picture with the caption 'Have you seen this man?' The Identikit photograph bore, even after two years, a striking resemblance to the heir of Rhuda.

All over Inverloch it was that indeterminate half hour or so when guests fill in the time before the call for dinner. Emile Casini was sitting in the hotel lounge, a chess board open before him. He was concentrating on an endgame problem in the Sunday paper folded neatly beside the board. Dempster entered the room, Bill Murray's *Mountaineering in Scotland* tucked under his arm. He noticed Casini deep in thought and came up behind him noiselessly.

"Bishop to Knight 5. Mate," he said politely after a few minutes.

"I believe you are right." Casini mastered his irritation and turned round. "That game of Fischer's started with the Sicilian

Defence." He indicated the newspaper he had been studying. "Very appropriate."

"Do you play chess much, Hugh?"

"Not now," Dempster admitted truthfully. "Life is too short for chess these days."

Casini's tongue made his distinctive clicking noise of disagreement. "Let us hope not, let us hope not."

Jim Atkinson was bored. He sat at a table in the square dining room of the Western Atlantic Hotel and gazed absently out over the ocean. A solidly built varnished Scottish trawler was heading north with the resilience of a sturdy pup. At least it was getting somewhere. Jim had been at the hotel for several days without very much to occupy him beyond routine calls to the Centre. When Swartze had told him he was to stand by to do anything Hugh Spencer wanted, he'd known better than to ask questions. But the sum total of activity on that front had been one parcel delivery to Inverness.

He had heard earlier, in the bar, about the *Celtic Pioneer* launch. Recently the talk had been about the death of a lobster fisherman who turned out to be an instructor in the Marines. Something unlikely and violent seemed to be going on somewhere, but not near him.

Two men walked into the dining room. The place was getting busier. He recognised one of the men as a scientist from the *Celtic Pioneer*. What was his name — quite a senior man. Wilson — yes, a geologist or a geophysicist or something. Wilson glanced his way and nodded briefly. Jim Atkinson acknowledged him with a slight movement of the hand. The man with Wilson was spare and sallow, with a rather long nose. He looked tired and had a worried expression, as if he had heard ill of the dinner menu. They sat down together in a large bay window on the far side of the room.

At the Point House Bernadino was looking at a comic. Though he couldn't read English he gave the odd chuckle, which to Jane Stewart sounded like the noise of someone moving a heavy table over a wooden floor.

She brought two large plates of garlic-smelling stew from the stove, slapped one down before her husband, and another before the Spaniard. As she leant round him he reached up and grasped her breast through the tight fitting sweater.

"You bastard, let go." She twisted away, her face flushed with anger. Bernadino merely chuckled again, took up his fork and resumed his comic. Across the table her husband had half risen from his chair, his knuckles showing white where he gripped his knife and fork.

"One of these days, Bernadino, you will go too far," he spat out. "We can only stand so much."

"But I can stand much of your wife, Meester Stewart," the Spaniard laughed, dipping his fork in his food. "And you can't get rid of me yet." He grinned up at Jane Stewart. "Stew very good. I like."

"You're nothing but a bloody animal." She glared at the two men. "How much longer do I have to stay here with this monster? Why don't you shoot the man, if you're too weak to hit him?"

The dining room at the Stob Dearg was almost full. The fishing party appeared to be having some kind of celebration. Several tables had been placed together and bottles of wine were strategically spaced. McCallum was in evening dress. He came over beaming to Cliff and devoured Tania with undressing eyes as he shepherded them superfluously to their usual table. When he had waddled off to fetch the wine, the highlights of his patent leather shoes winking, Tania turned to Cliff and shivered.

"I can't stop thinking about the fact that there's someone walking round Inverloch tonight who tried to kill us this morning."

Dempster drank soup.

"I know Paul Wilson is suspect number one, but I just can't see him doing something like that," Tania continued.

"No. I rather think he has a quieter line all together."

"Then there're those Anglo-Italian people out at the Point House that Alasdair was telling us about."

"Friends of friend Casini."

"And he's not the only oil man in the hotel."

"The fishermen? Yes, I had intended having an innocent chat with them tonight, but I doubt if they're going to stay perpendicular long enough." The fishing group was becoming progressively noisier as the meal advanced. Two helpings of rock cod appeared, drowned in McCallum's best wine sauce.

"Casini's afternoon alibi," grinned Cliff. " 'Gone fishing' ."

"Tell me more about Alasdair MacAlasdair," Tania said. "Have you known him a long time?"

"Yes, years, in fact."

"Did you know he was up here?" Dempster told her how he had found his friend and gave her a brief account of the severed hand and the significance of where Alasdair had found it. The coffee arrived and they were silent for a while.

"I think I might pay a visit to the police," Cliff said eventually.

"Is that wise?"

"Nothing to lose. And despite what Alasdair says, they do seem to be hot-footing it about these days. They're obviously still interested in Aqua John."

"I thought he was run down by another boat?"

"That's the accepted theory, yes."

"But you and Alasdair think differently?"

"Uhuh."

"And you actually think John Pollock's death could be connected with the McBrides and Rhuda?"

"Could be."

"Are you going to give that hand to the police?"

"Probably will eventually. But at present I just want to have a casual little chat. I don't want them swarming under my feet, which they would if they knew where Alasdair found the thing. At the moment I want to be helped not hampered by the strong arm of the law."

The strong arm of the law, in the shape of Inspector Charlie Galloway, was *not* engaged in eating dinner. He was on the afternoon shift which meant two to ten pm, and gazing thoughtfully at the memo on his desk. It was a report phoned in by the coastguard about a launch sunk off Gruinard Bay. Lying beside the memo was a report from Ullapool about various people's movements. The matters didn't appear to be obviously related. PC MacCormack's brief report indicated that a certain individual had been watching the movements of the Consolidated Oil's giant tanker, *Black Harvest*, through powerful binoculars from a ridge above Gruinard Bay. There was no mention in the report of the sinking of the launch. Charlie Galloway sighed, and didn't waste time adding an obvious two and two. He reached for the telephone.

"Get me PC MacKay at Inverloch, would you, Alf?"

"Great meal." Dempster nodded to McCallum as they met in the foyer. "We're just going outside for a breather."

"I'm surprised that you managed to eat at all after your experiences today, Miss Olsen." The proprietor beamed. "You must have fantastic powers of recovery."

"It must be your good food, Mr McCallum."

"Were the fishing group having a farewell dinner tonight?" Cliff asked.

"No, but one of them landed a nice salmon today. They have a wager on that anyone catching a ten-pounder or over has to pay for the wine."

"Rather takes the edge off the sport, doesn't it?" asked Tania.

"Not at all," McCallum laughed. "These oilmen…"

"I think I'd like to meet them," Dempster sounded interested. "Nothing like picking brains, even if they are on holiday. Can you tell me which of them are in the oil business?"

"Let me see, now, there's Mr Marples, that's the baldheaded one with the deep voice, and Mr Edgeware, him in the tartan trews. He's something to do with pipelines. He organised the contract with the Japs for the David's Head refinery, I believe."

"Interesting man."

"Well, you'd better start the conversation rolling about fish," warned McCallum. "They have a thing about talking shop amongst themselves."

Outside the sun was low in the sky and the whole village was bathed in a golden light. Several holidaymakers were standing gazing raptly out over the harbour wall, the less romantically inclined were striding toward the public bar which was situated at the extreme westerly end of the hotel, almost opposite the pier.

Casini came through the double doors, casually dressed in a black anorak and dark trousers, a cigarette glowed in his mouth. His eyes swept the seafront and came to rest on Tania and Dempster. He sauntered over, walking with the precise delicacy of a ballet dancer.

"What a wonderful evening," he murmured. "It reminds me of home. I come from just such a little fishing village in the south of Sicily."

"Just look at Stob Dearg" said Tania. "It's deep purple."

"That reminds me," Dempster said, "I was speaking to Paul Wilson. He has some climbing plans lined up for us." He looked up the distant rock face. Lilley's route could still just be traced on the flank.

"Then we must get ourselves into training for this young man. Perhaps you would care to come out with me for that hill-walking we promised ourselves, Tania?" Casini suggested. "I'm sure Mr Spencer will be able to manage on his own for one day."

"Perfectly," Cliff replied evenly. "Why don't you go the day after tomorrow? I have to visit the platform yard and you know that will be very boring for you, Tania."

Tania glanced sharply at him.

"Well," she deliberated. "If Emile is kind enough to ask me, and you don't need me, I'll gladly accept."

"Good," Dempster went on briskly. "Then you can take me over to Strathcon in the morning and pick me up when you return."

"That is good. I am putting my car in for an oil change. And I will cancel an appointment I have with a large, unknown salmon." Casini laughed.

"There's an easy way up Stob Dearg from the side," Cliff offered helpfully.

"Excellent. Now if you both will excuse me, I have been standing still all day and have promised myself a walk. This morning I tried to lure salmon, alas with no success. The rock cod this afternoon — I know they are not the same thing — but I catch them."

"Where did you try for salmon?" Dempster asked.

"Oh, here and there on the Coen, but the water is very low."

"Well, we enjoyed the fish tremendously," Tania said warmly.

"Perhaps you will shortly also enjoy my salmon. Until tomorrow." He bowed politely and turned to walk lightly off up the street.

"When I want to get a date with a man, I can usually manage to do it on my own, you know," said Tania icily.

Cliff chuckled and took her arm to return to the hotel. "Think how pleased your Mr Swartze will be," he told her. "He's getting two special investigators for the price of one."

13

FOR MANY YEARS the house of Rhuda had adhered to a rigid timetable. Agnes produced amazingly uninspired and unappetising meals with monotonous regularity. At 7.30 pm dinner was served and, like well-trained mice, all those in residence meekly took their places. It would be the same, James thought, if he hadn't come back for another fifty years. It required too great an effort to defy Agnes.

The family later assembled round the drawing room fire drinking coffee, mercifully made by Caren. Hector McBride drained his brandy, stood with a grimace and limped stiffly toward the door.

"I think I'll go down and have a cast at the sea pool. Either of you two coming?" He clutched the door with one talon and regarded his children through pale eyes.

"May take a stroll down before I go to bed," Caren answered, helping herself to a chocolate from the box on the mantelpiece. "Will it be any use?"

"Quite possibly. We've kept those damned tourists off the Bhan for several weeks. There're still the poachers, of course. But both Alec and Johnny say there's a big one at the pool."

"But Alec told me you've been after that fish for ages, Pop. Why don't you wait for more water?"

"That fish has got all the water it needs, Caren. It's just reluctant to take the lure."

"What are you fishing, Dad?" James asked.

"I was trying a Black Dose," his father replied. "But I'm not sure. Johnny has made up one of his specials for me, a Silver Wilkinson with triple hooks."

"Well, let me know if you hook it," grinned James. "And I'll give you a hand."

"I'm still quite capable of landing the biggest salmon that these rivers can produce, thank you," replied the Laird with dignity, as he limped from the room.

Johnny Bhan had a touch of wind that evening. He always suffered when he ate too much venison. Though the hind season had passed, his wife Caroline made good use of the freezer.

"I think I'll go down and have a spy at the river — see if the old man's had any luck," Johnny remarked as he rose from the table.

"Him and that salmon of his." She began washing up in the small kitchenette.

"Aye, it's a big beast. Must be all of forty-five pounds. The biggest I've seen in these parts."

Two poachers, as well known to the police and the bailiffs as to their own wives, were having a quiet drink in the pub in Inverloch.

"I think we'll take a holiday for a wee while, Dochy. The water's a bit warm at present."

"You're right, man. We'll need to bide our time. Those keepers up at Rhuda will be cramming carrots down their gullets every teatime, so they don't happen to miss us. Hey, Donald, another couple of pints here."

Hector McBride moved out along the narrow spit of limestone which protruded fifteen feet into the centre of the peat-coloured pool. Stunted birches grew on the banks. Adapted to Arctic conditions, they thrived on the exposed coast of Rhuda. The name sea pool was a misnomer, as even on the highest tide the sea never reached this far, but it had the name by virtue of being the first major pool from the mouth of the river.

As a child, McBride had accompanied his father onto this spit of rock; it was where he had caught his first salmon. He had never forgotten the initial thrill, now almost sixty-five years ago, and the dynamic power of the fighting fish — it had been a real tussle. He assembled the rod with deliberation and the ease of long practice; then thoughtfully glanced over the pool. He thought of starting off with a Jock Scott fly, for the night had an edge to it, but finally decided against it and tied the Silver Wilkinson to the fifteen-pound tapered cast. Some fresh clouds had promised rain. It could be an advantage, he thought; a wee smear wouldn't do any damage. He had brought his oilskins, but a bit of rain never did anyone any harm.

A feeling of tranquillity stole over him as he took the first gentle cast, testing the water, gradually working out to a likely spot he knew of old: a little eddy in the peat-dark water, just the faintest of ripples there, not a bubble or a bit of froth on the water, yet a breeze sufficient to ruffle it ever so slightly. He cast again, the fly falling like a tuft of down from a passing duck, gently kissing the water as if, at the point of landing, it had almost changed its mind...

It was nearly midnight when Caren collected her coat and followed her father's route slowly along the rocky shore towards the river mouth. A freshening breeze was blowing over Inchmhor Island from across a sea whose farther shore was Labrador. She remembered what her brother had told her of an African tribe who called the sea a big river with only one bank. That was nice, she decided, only one bank. It suggested infinity.

Other eyes, too, were busy in the area that night, but they were not speculating on infinity, or the Atlantic.

From a hillock upstream on the far bank Johnny Bhan was able to look down on the Auld Bastard, as he and Alec sometimes referred to their employer. Caren watched her father absently from a promontory three hundred feet away. She didn't want to go closer and disturb him and she was absorbed in her own thoughts. The time drifted past.

Suddenly the fisherman's angular frame shifted. With a stifled cry of surprise McBride fell sideways from the finger of rock into the deep and silent black water of the sea pool. On the far bank Johnny didn't have a very clear view — his eyes had been glued to McBride's rod. But he saw the rod drop as the Auld

109

Bastard plunged into the water, his arms outspread in a helpless fashion. For one paralysed moment, neither watcher moved; then, with a strangled gulp, Caren ran down the narrow path towards her father. Johnny moved with surprising agility, and wasn't far behind Caren as she reached the pool.

"Quick!" she commanded. "He's surfaced." The keeper jumped into the water downstream — it came high up his plus-fours, but he knew there was a shallow shelf about four feet below the surface. A soggy tweed jacket came into view, like a saturated sack, and the limp edge of a kilt. He grabbed the jacket and towed the listless body ashore. Together, they dragged the old man onto a flat rock, face downwards, and attempted to drain his lungs by tilting him. They applied mouth to mouth, and cardiac massage for an hour before they finally desisted and acknowledged defeat. The Laird was dead.

"Any more thoughts on your shipwreck?" Alasdair and Cliff were waiting in the cottage for it to be late enough for their nocturnal excursion.

"Not really. I think we're agreed that the explosion was activated by the starter button, aren't we?"

"Makes sense. If it was primed the morning you left, that would be the most logical way. That's the way I would do it, as an engineer."

"Which means, then, that whoever set it knew the speed of the launch, and had a good knowledge of the currents and tides."

"And who would that be? Paul Wilson?"

"I doubt it. I have my doubts whether he even knows what I'm doing here. He's very much a greenhorn at this sort of thing. But James McBride may have rumbled me, of all people." Cliff explained about the letter he had intercepted and also his visit to Paul Wilson's cabin. "He had this map of Rhuda hidden away in a real boy-scout location, and a newspaper cutting which he's obviously using to put the screws on young McBride."

"To do what?"

"Presumably to persuade his old man to dispose of the family's fallen estate in a way highly beneficial to Paul Wilson."

"Huh. I can't see James McBride persuading father to do

anything father doesn't want to. His old man can bend him like a safety pin."

"I wonder. Say, is that A.J.'s airgun?" Cliff pointed to the CO_2 underwater gun which was propped in the corner of the room. Several steel arrows lay beside it.

"Yes, I must send it down to his mother. I suppose I should have given it to the police when they were here, but one doesn't think…"

"How about you drawing me a rough plan of the Point House, to put me in the picture?" Cliff suggested.

"Sure." Alasdair reached up to the mantelpiece for a pencil and took a scrap of paper. With precise lines he drew a map of the house and the point, then turned it and explained to Cliff.

"It's a big place, quite modern, brick rendered with white Torrin marble. Built for a retired admiral. There's an annexe, here, from the east wing which runs down from this gable end and almost meets up with the boathouse on a higher level. The boathouse, where they keep that classy cutter I was telling you about, is down here, built into the cliff face. A tidy job."

"How much ground is there?"

"Not much. Four acres, at the most, I would say." Alasdair outlined the area on his map. "The lawn — that's in the front," he stabbed with his pencil, "runs level for about forty feet to the north, I guess." He paused, reflecting. "Then it dips down to a low sandstone cliff and the water. Rhodies grow all over the shop, and there's a clump of Wellingtonia about here." He drew a symbolic pine tree on the map. "There's a flagpole about here," he put a cross in front of the house, just across the drive.

Cliff glanced at his watch.

"I suppose we could make a move… Can you take us to the Point via the sewers, or similar?"

"I'll take you a devious route which lessens our chance of being spotted, at any rate," he laughed. "It's a throwback from having misspent my youth here. I got to know all the dodges!"

The road leading to the Point terminated at the house, but a locked gate at the boundary wall prevented public access to the grounds. Here the neck of land which formed the point was at its narrowest; on their left was Lochan Beag, the sheltered bay

111

where Cliff had seen the Spanish trawler when he first arrived. They could see lights still blazing in the hotel lounge; the fishing club were still hard at it, no doubt.

"I think we'll approach on the right from the shore," Alasdair decided. "Make for the boathouse." They picked their way along the boulders until they merged into a cliff which overhung deeper water. Then they moved up the bank and reached the wall that ran right down to the cliff edge. Three new strands of barbed wire, on steel stanchions, added considerably to its height, and it took them a couple of minutes to climb over. Skirting the rhododendrons, they reached the boathouse where bushes overhung the twenty foot rock face. There were no lights showing in the house. The water below them glimmered like pitch. The dark margin of a chain of rocks could faintly be discerned to their left, protecting the small harbour thus formed. Alasdair hadn't realised it was so sheltered; it certainly didn't look it from the sea. The back door of the boathouse was locked and it wasn't easy to gain entrance via the sea-facing doors as the corners had steel spikes built into the brickwork, in an ornamental but effective way. Cliff fiddled with the door and very soon it swung open. Alasdair waited outside whilst he had a quick look round.

There was no boat. The place was empty, except for some tackle and a few drums of lubricating oil. The main sea doors of the building were open. A large fuel tank had been built into the brick wall at the sea entrance; he estimated that it would hold about 3,000 gallons. He closed the door behind him with just a faint click.

"Anything?" whispered Alasdair.

"Nope. The boat's out, too. I think we'd better wait and see if Stewart and Co. turn up. Let's make ourselves comfortable." They both dozed lightly in the centre of a clump of rhododendrons, but had not been waiting long before the low throb of engines brought them instantly wide awake.

"That's it now," breathed Alasdair. The throttle was shut back. They could just see the long, low lines as the cutter approached. "This I must see — I'd give a fiver to any man who could take that boat in through these rocks at night." Barely pausing, the sleek craft came on in the darkness, as unerringly as a bat.

"That's a fiver you owe Stewart," Cliff whispered a few moments later. She was right below them, nosing her way into the boathouse entrance like an enormous shark. Lights shone as she glided inside and the engines were silenced.

"I wouldn't have believed that! She's got radar, but..."

There was a double thud as the heavy boathouse doors were closed, and a grating noise of a securing bar being pulled into place. Muffled footsteps, then the rear door of the boathouse opened, followed by the now familiar click of it closing. Footfalls could be heard on the concrete path. One of the party cleared his throat loudly and spat. Another made a similar sort of noise, but neither spoke. They stopped, apparently, before they reached the gravel at the front door. Cliff could have sworn that one man detached himself from the others and sidled off. A minute or so later, the front door latch clicked in place and a discreet sliver of light was seen presently in the front room window.

They waited for twenty minutes. No further movement or unusual noise was detected.

"Did they all go in?" Cliff whispered.

"I don't think so, but I guess the other was visiting."

"I'll go back to the boathouse, Alasdair," Cliff decided. "Keep your eyes skinned." The burly Scotsman took up a position close to the top of the steps, which gave him a worm's eye view of the approach from the house. It would be difficult for anybody to catch him completely unawares. Cliff took only a few minutes to open the door. He pulled it close silently. His pencil torch cast eerie shadows onto the corrugated roof of the building. The cutter filled its berth with only a few inches to spare either side of the concrete 'U'. He shone the torch slowly over the boat and its beam rested on the wheelhouse door.

Cliff stepped on board and tried the door; it was locked. Bending down to inspect it, he discovered that it was a modern multi-lever lock which would take some time to crack, so he moved to the forward hatch. It was padlocked but, despite its formidable appearance, the brass padlock yielded quickly and he eased the hatch cover back. The torch's concentrated beam stabbed the interior: it was a large hold, the front part forming the chain locker; a stout wooden partition formed a bulkhead. The hold itself was half-filled with cordage and some bulky kitbags. He could see also a small Baur compressor, and several air cylinders, painted black. He dropped inside and opened a bag; then let out a silent whistle. Rebreathing gear — Italian. What the hell? It was still wet. Another bag contained several boxes of gelignite, whilst a well-padded box held detonators. Two heavy underwater compressed air guns — the type used for shark and big game fish — were lying on one side, and about twenty steel-tipped arrows. He replaced these items as he had found them and pulled himself back up through the hatch. He fitted the cover again and relocked the padlock; then returned to the wheelhouse. Shining the torch through the wide screen, he could see at a glance that she was extremely well equipped: an automatic pilot close to the wheel behind which, on a ledge which obviously also served as a bunk, was a Decca Navigator. The paper from an echo sounder hung down; the last tracings were still visible on the recording paper. They fluctuated from 5-15 fathoms, then back to 5; close to the machine they indicated 7 fathoms. He made a mental note to study the charts. He found also the usual radio paraphernalia, including a directional finder and radar. What interested him most was a binocular instrument, mounted at eye level on a single rod located in the facia in front of the wheel. Obviously an oversight that it had been left on the locating mount, it was by no means standard equipment. Dempster recognised it as a Barr and Stroud CU viewer — one of the most powerful night viewers on the market. It became clear to him how Stewart had taken the boat in so unerringly; it had been, quite literally, as bright as day. The cost of that little bauble would by itself purchase a fair-sized boat. He decided he had seen enough and made his way back to his faithful watchdog.

As they paused to climb back over the wall, Dempster felt, more than saw, the shadow up by the main gate. He touched his friend's arm and they both froze. "Someone there"

Alasdair strained his eyes, but could see nothing. Eventually,

Dempster touched his sleeve and they moved off, down to the cover of the margin of shore.

"Well?" Alasdair asked, when they were back safely in his cottage. "What was that flap about?"

"I think it was one of the midnight cruise party interested in our peregrinations."

"Oh? I didn't see a thing."

"There was someone all right, and I'd like to know who it was. There's something niggling in my mind, Alasdair... something we heard."

"We hardly heard a darned thing. Have some coffee." Alasdair offered him an old china mug.

"Thanks."

"Find anything else in the boathouse?"

"Plenty." Cliff elaborated.

At Rhuda House the mirrors were covered, an old Highland custom, and the blinds half drawn. It had taken Agnes some time to perform this task, as some of them hadn't been disturbed for years. The stretched out body of the late Hector McBride lay stiffer, if this were possible, than it had in his lifetime.

It was after two am before Alec and Johnny had put the body on an old door and carried it back into the house. Dr McLeod, on being summoned by James, had declined to go down to the pool, for his back was bothering him.

"Weel," commented Trigger MacKay, who had arrived in time to assist during the latter stages of the cortege, "I'm glad that's over. I'll leave you to finish your examination Dr McLeod, and pop in to see you before I go."

"Aye, that's fine, Constable. Fifteen minutes at the outside."

Before intruding on the family, Trigger decided to have a word below stairs, and as he had hoped found a cup of tea waiting in the huge kitchen, where Alec and Johnny were taking something stronger. It was agreed that it was a sad night for Rhuda. But it was also agreed with equal vehemence that being a bearer party was thirsty work. Johnny explained once again what had happened and Trigger wrote things down in his notebook.

115

"He just seemed to fall in sideways, with a kind of helpless cry."

"Did he have a bite from that salmon of his maybe?"

"No, no," Alec put in scornfully. "He was far too old a hand to be caught unawares like that."

"I've been thinking, it could have been his brogues," offered Johnny, nursing his dram. "The rock down by the pool is fearfully slippery. He usually wore his waders, you see. But it was dry tonight, so I suppose he didn't bother."

"That may well be." Trigger consulted his notebook. "I see one of his shoes was missing." He snapped the book shut and rose with more energy than he had evinced hitherto. "Well now, I'll just pop up and have a look at the gunroom to see that everything's in order while I'm here."

"The old man wasn't shot, you know," Alec answered shortly. He had remembered that he had neglected to clean the bolt of a .275 as well as he ought.

"At least it'll save you coming back in a couple of week's time!"

"Aye, well, we'll see about that," replied the constable noncommittally at the door.

"It's like being in the army having that bugger around. He's worse than that old arms sergeant I had at Aldershot, and he was bad enough, by Christ."

"If you're going to use language like that in my kitchen, you can just take yourself outside, Alec Dubh." Agnes turned on him. "It's a disgrace with the master not yet cold."

"Oh, he's cold enough," said Johnny. "Mark my words."

14

Sandy, the chef at the Stob Dearg, was known locally as the Blood. This was on account of his cutting himself regularly when carving the meat in an inebriated state. He hadn't been to bed at all that night and swayed as he went along the passageway to the kitchen. He remembered vaguely putting a couple of cans of Export in the fridge the previous day. The kiosk telephone rang as he went past, and swivelling on one foot he opened the door in a single movement and lifted the receiver. The slick action was spoilt by his trying to speak into the earpiece. Eventually he heard a voice asking for a guest called Mr Spencer. "What bloody time…" he started, and dropped the receiver. It hung from its cord, banging against the glass. Mumbling obscurely Sandy realigned himself for the stairs and staggered up them with the good if imprecise intention of rousing a guest. One seemed much the same as another, as far as he was concerned.

Dempster felt that his head had only just hit the pillow when he heard someone lurching against his door and rub on along the corridor. He grabbed his bathrobe and investigated. Sandy was peering and weaving at Tania's door, hopefully waiting for his deductive powers to catch up with his feet.

"Lost something?" Cliff asked.

"Ah!" The chef swivelled his head round, as if it were on ball bearings. "Telephone." Mission accomplished, he beamed and tacked back to the head of the stairs. Cliff followed, bemused, and was not any less puzzled to find the voice at the end of the dangling handset belonged to Alasdair.

"Alasdair? What's up?"

"Old McBride drowned in his salmon pool last night." Alasdair didn't believe in mincing words.

"How?" Cliff was equally abrupt.

"Fell in, with Caren and one of the keepers looking on. Caren phoned me."

"All above board, then?"

"Seems to be." Alasdair didn't sound too positive. "Caren's worried, though, about something."

"Must have been a bit of a shock."

"Yes, but apart from that. Anyway, I'm going over to see her later when, you know, all the business is over. I wondered whether you and Tania wanted to come too?"

"Okay. How about meeting her at the Bhan Bridge, say two-thirty?"

"Fine for me. I'll let you know if Caren can't manage it."

Dempster lay on the top of his bed for a couple of hours, thinking. When he got up he saw from his window Casini and the other two oil men, Marples and Edgeware, putting fishing rods into a Volvo estate. Edgeware was wearing startling Clan McIntosh tartan trousers with a cap to match. Marples was absorbed in explaining something to Casini. He watched them drive away.

On an impulse he switched off his razor and went along the corridor to the Sicilian's room. It was locked, but his section of wire soon opened it, and Cliff slipped quickly inside. Rapidly he conducted a search, but in minutes he instinctively knew that he was frisking the room of another professional. There was nothing other than one could expect: fishing tackle, some climbing gear and a large selection of expensive clothes.

It was Annie who delivered the mail in Inverloch. People of both sexes referred to her as Annie the Bag. Those with a charitable disposition credited this to the large canvas sack in which she transported the post. It had been manufactured some eleven years previously in Her Majesty's Prison, Peterhead. On

118

a heavy day, as she described it, when there was a large delivery, Annie was forced to take Peter's old bike with its sturdy carrier. But the machine was really only suited to wheeling, as the crossbar demanded excessive exposure of her prodigious pink thighs, albeit sheathed in heavy no-nonsense stockings during the winter. Annie was a widow, a generous woman. Since the death of her husband, Willie McPhail, a lobster fisherman, she had had a surplus of affection and surprisingly few inhibitions. The Stob Dearg mail was in a bundle held together by the regulation post office elastic band. The topmost envelope of the pile had a green Special Delivery sticker and a motif of a microscope on the upper left-hand corner. Underneath, in small print, were the words Scientific Laboratories Ltd. The letter was addressed to H. Spencer, Esq. Annie arrived rather breathless in Reception and laid the mail on Morag's counter.

"That's your lot today," she announced. Morag left her typewriter where there was a half finished copy of the day's menu.

"Thank's Annie. Another fine morning."

"Aye, it is that. But not so good for old McBride."

"McBride?"

"Aye, the Laird himself. Fell into his salmon pool last night, and snuffed it."

"My, that's terrible." Morag was round eyed. "Mr McCallum will be most upset to hear that."

"Aye, Dochy at the shop was telling me there was a fearful big salmon in that pool. I think he and Archie the Toad were keen on it."

"Was he pulled in, then?"

"Aye, I think so. Donnie Carmichael was speaking on the phone with Alec Dubh this morning about his daughter. She's going down to Dingwall next term to stay with Donnie's sister, Mary. Alec told him that he'd found the Laird's rod but the hook was gone, and the gaff is missing as well."

"My!" Morag repeated again, "that's the second death in a week, Annie."

"Aye, I don't know what the place is coming to." Annie

119

nodded complacently and shouldered her bag — she didn't like leaving it unattended on the bicycle.

Another drowning, thought Charlie Galloway. Less than a mile away from the last. No doubt about old McBride, thank goodness. Two witnesses saw the old boy fall into his favourite salmon pool. There'd be a big funeral for the Laird. He wondered who'd get the estate. McBride had a son, he remembered, but Charlie didn't think much of him. Not the same grit as the old man. But the girl, now, was bonnie enough. Aye, a bonnie lassie...

Charlie was driving up the A296 to Inverloch and Rhuda. Beside him in the car sat Detective Constable Tom Nicholson.

"It's a great way to die," Charlie voiced his thoughts aloud. "A ripe old age, making a last cast in your favourite pool." Charlie himself — though by no means an addict — was known to enjoy the odd day on a Highland river, with just himself, a rod, and the open sky. It gave him a sense of perspective, of the smallness of himself and the futility of time.

"Aye, it's a grand way to go," agreed Tom, a large overgrown man who had run to fat, though he was hard enough beneath, having spent his early years shepherding on the hill country of Sutherland. Formerly he'd been as lean as a stoat, but found the police life somewhat indolent in comparison. "I'd rather go with one on the jigger, though," he added with a smile.

"You teuchters are all the same," Charlie laughed. "A salmon holds the same attraction for you as a new hat to the missus!"

"Aye," Tom continued in a mock philosophic vein. "Fly means or foul, but we usually reckon there's more fun in the foul..."

"The keepers think he slipped because he was wearing heavy brogues, with those triple hobs. I must say they've always seemed a ridiculous form of footwear to me — I don't know why more of them don't turn their ankles — "

"There's nothing to beat a good pair of the old 'Herd Laddies'." Tom waxed enthusiastic on the subject of hill footwear. "Wi' a wee bit o' whale oil on them; it makes them fine and waterproof. We used to use it for suppling the tits of the

120

ewes, and they never gave any bother... Just used to oil them twice a year, I did."

"Aye, that's what the old bugger should have been wearing last night," muttered Charlie. "It would have saved us a journey this morning. I've got a shinty match on at five o'clock and I'll have to flog the arse off this old heap to get back in time. But the Chief wants us to pay our respects by having a wee interested look."

"Is Trigger meeting us?"

"Yes, he'll be up at the house. He was there a good bit o' the night, I gather." Charlie's attention was abruptly diverted by the sight of one of his personal bêtes noires, a car and caravan parked on a treacherous bend. The owner, a fat bespectacled man, was taking a photograph of the river with the hills beyond. Charlie blared his horn and flashed the blue light. Fatso beamed at the acknowledgment as they flew past.

"If I'd had time, I'd have stopped and torn a strip off that bastard. If they only knew what we have to suffer each year with them and their caravans..."

"John Bowden, in Traffic, calls it the annual thrombosis syndrome," replied Tom, well pleased that he had successfully got his tongue round the words.

Hughie the Hearse mused. He stared blankly down at the printed card in front of him. It bore the sombre title 'Funeral Arrangements' and below the tasteful gothic lettering it ran:

Name	Place of Interment
Age	Notices
Died	Sign. on Notices
Address	Dimensions
Solicitors	Shroud
Next of Kin	Hires
Telephone	Wreaths
Day of Funeral	Advertisements
Lair(s)	Doctor
Minister	

To one side of the card waas a finely bound Bible with a well-thumbed look. Beside the Bible was a miniature coffin with gilded handles. Hughie kept his pen and pencil in this, as he didn't like unseemly clutter on his desk.

Hugh Donaldson operated his funeral business with the solemnity the profession demanded. Not ever darkening the doorway of a public house, certainly not locally, unless it was for the removal of the late owner, or one of his dependents. This was not to imply that Hughie wasn't partial to a dram; far from it! One night per week, he would lock himself in the front room, directly above the funeral parlour, with a bottle of malt and become 'miraculous', as they say in the Highlands. During his at home, as he termed it, his wife would go to the bingo, a pastime for which she had a deep-rooted passion, almost as urgent as Hughie's need for the bottle.

As a legacy of these tippling devotions, Hughie had acquired a florid colouring which would extend to the very top of his bald head on a winter's day in a windswept graveyard. In an effort to combat this hue, so unbecoming in his profession, his wife insisted on powdering his face and dome before any important engagement. By dint of years of practice, opening his jaws slightly and keeping his lips closed in a tight pale line, his eyes as expressionless as glass marbles, Hughie could portray a cadaverous expression to perfection. The aroma of formalin followed him around like pungent after-shave.

Hughie had taken over his father's empty coffins a number of years before when his old man had been put under ground by the opposition — a part-time undertaker, his father's one-time rival. However, the job had been done at trade rates and, since that day, Hughie had called on Bill Mechie's assistance from time to time. They were often to be seen riding side by side in Hughie's highly polished Austin hearse, like two pale waxen images, their customer ensconced behind in solitary splendour.

Few if any undertakers die laughing, but they do invariably have a keen sense of humour. Hughie and Bill would exchange jokes without even moving their lips as they drove sedately towards their destination. Subsequent laughter was accomplished with the mouth slightly open and eyes fixed straight ahead, achieving a facial expression which must have been taken as one of silent prayer by the casual observer. Hughie's father, too, had a fine sense of humour. Though it was apparently a mistake when the following advert appeared in the *West Highland Gazette and Advertiser* fifteen years earlier: 'Hearse for sale — good running order; body in need of repair.'

Hughie had been summoned to Rhuda that day. The old chap would need tidying up, he thought, and the Last Services were always a bonus. He had laid McBride's late wife to rest: 5' 9" x 16" — he remembered the coffin size well. Hughie took his job seriously; he knew McBride's size, as he knew that of sixty others whose custom would eventually come his way. The old bugger would need a twenty-inch coffin, he estimated. He would suggest the oak job with the walled panels. Hughie was inclined to enthuse, in a very sombre way, naturally, over the arrangements. McBride wouldn't be wanting a shroud, he thought. They always got buried in their kilts, these gentry... Pity, though, that was a bonnie shroud he had in stock, with the wee bow tie. Hughie's pale lips were compressed in a thin line. He hadn't sold a casket for a long time, he realised. A good profit margin on a real work of art, he thought fondly of the oak hooped model with the full-length barrel handles. Ah, it would be a pleasure to be laid to rest in one of them.

His thoughts flew ahead now. He would have to remember to tell old Archie to put some sods and soil in first this time. Mrs McBride's coffin was almost smashed by those rocks, and it echoed like a drum, as if there had been nothing inside at all.

Alasdair and Caren were standing by the river under a large silver birch, looking out towards the sea, when Cliff and Tania arrived at Rhuda that afternoon. Caren had dark circles under her eyes, but she seemed to be in control of herself and accepted their expressions of sympathy and concern calmly.

"The police left here just before lunch," she reported. "There was an inspector and another man, a sergeant, I think."

"I saw Trigger as well," added Alasdair. "Met him on the road on the way from the village."

"They seemed quite satisfied." Caren gazed pensively at the

river. The bank was high and she stared down into the dark water. "But I'm worried, there's something wrong somewhere that I can't quite put my finger on."

All four walked in silence down the wooded bank until they reached the point where she had been standing the previous night. It was a peaceful scene. The water ran down the rocks to the left and entered a deep pool. Beyond, it flowed faster, hurrying down this last reach to the open sea. The river mouth was hidden from where they were standing, but they could see the Atlantic stretching beyond.

"Could you bear to go through it again for me?" Cliff asked diffidently.

"He was fishing from that rock spit," she pointed, "casting diagonally, slightly left, looking downstream. I was watching from here. The light wasn't good, but I could see him quite clearly. He just gave a cry and pitched sideways."

"Did you manage to make out the words he said?"

"No. It was nothing intelligible, just a cry of...of surprise, really."

"Did he slip, do you think?"

"It's impossible to tell. One moment he was there, fishing, and the next he was under the water."

"How long was he submerged?" Cliff asked reluctantly. He knew she must be feeling the strain of the day's events. Caren thought for a moment, then replied in a low voice.

"The Inspector asked me the same question and I said that I thought he came up right away, but I've been thinking again and I'm not so sure. You see, I ran down from here to the spit and he had surfaced before Johnny Bhan reached me a few moments later. But he could have come up before that. It would have been difficult for me to see, as I was running. I went down to the left from here, then back parallel with the bank until I reached the spit, and the rock itself would have hidden his body until I was nearly there."

"Was he face down when you got to him?"

"Yes. It was a bit of a struggle to pull him out. He only had one shoe," she added inconsequentially as the desolate details crowded back.

124

"And you couldn't revive him?"

"No, we tried for ages, but it was no good." Her eyes clouded as she relived the previous night.

"Lay off, Cliff," Alasdair said fiercely. "She's had about enough. The keeper saw it all too. You can talk to him."

"Yes, he was standing on the other bank." Caren pointed to the promontory on the far side of the river at the bottom of the field below Johnny's cottage. Then she showed them exactly where her father had been standing.

"When he fell, Caren, did you notice what happened to the rod?" Cliff asked.

"It fell in front of him. And his gaff. Alec Dubh got them this morning, further down stream. On the right, just past that bend down there. The hook and part of the cast were missing."

"So he might have got a bite," Alasdair thought aloud.

"Well, you can ask Johnny Bhan yourself," Caren replied. "He's up in the house right now, but he doesn't think so."

"Um," Dempster was thoughtful for a minute. "Well, it was very good of you to go over everything like this for me, Caren."

"That's all right. I've been over it so many times for the police already, I don't mind any more. But there's something, something I just can't place, something I had hoped would come back to me if I kept forcing myself to go over what had happened. You see, I just wouldn't have expected Dad to fall in like that, even though his arthritis was bad."

"Could he swim?"

"Yes. He was a reasonably good swimmer in his younger days. But he didn't seem to have a chance. Somehow or other, I got the impression that he was as surprised as I was. I just don't know…" she faltered, looking to Alasdair for moral support. "It simply doesn't add up."

Before Cliff and Tania returned to Inverloch, Alasdair introduced them to Johnny Bhan. The best fly maker in the West produced the Laird's fly book, but could add nothing material to the picture Caren had already painted.

"Caren tells me you don't think her father was pulled in by a salmon?" Cliff said.

"No. I told the Inspector that. And PC MacKay. I was

125

watching him closely, or his rod at least. I've good eyesight. You need to in my line of business. I'm sure he didn't get a bite. He just seemed to fall into the pool for no reason — no reason at all." The keeper pulled his fore and aft down at the front in a nervous way. "It's no' the sort of thing I would have expected to happen. The Laird was as strong as an ox, you know."

"Did you ever see that other chap who was killed diving at the river mouth?" Cliff changed the subject suddenly.

Johnny gave an uncertain glance at Alasdair. "He was a friend of yours, wasn't he?"

"He was."

"It was said he was poaching, but I doubt it. Yes, I saw him several times. Thought I saw you in your boat there, quite recently as well?"

"I've got a few creels out — seems a good place."

"Aye, strange too, with all that fresh water." Johnny turned to Dempster again. "I only saw him at a distance, mind, but the night he died the missus heard a motor in the wee hours. She couldn't tell from the noise what it was. It could have been an outboard, though."

"You've never seen anyone else diving out there, then?" Cliff asked him.

"No, I never did, but one night Alec was looking for otters and thought he saw something in the river mouth. But it could have been a seal. You seem very interested in the River Bhan, Mr Spencer." The keeper peered shrewdly up at Cliff.

"Like you, I'm a bit puzzled about things."

The talk in the bar before dinner that night was all of the death of the Laird of Rhuda. McCallum announced importantly that he would be attending the funeral. He thought gloomily of the custom he had had over the years from McBride's fishermen and how he would miss it.

"Lost one of your local worthies, eh?" Mr Marples said jovially. He was feeling in a convivial mood, having at last, after a great expense of money, hooked an eight-pound salmon.

"Is the funeral to be private?" enquired Morag.

"No, but he's being buried beside his wife in that little

kirkyard at Rhuda. It'll be a big event, if I'm not mistaken."

"I always recall Calchas, the soothsayer, when I think of death," volunteered Mr Marples with his invincible cheerfulness, including Cliff in his audience. As nobody asked him why, he continued, "He died of laughter, at the thought of having outlived the predicted hour of his death."

This appealed to McCallum's sense of humour, and he remembered his proprietorial duties to enquire after the fishing party's success. The oil man preened visibly as he described his salmon.

"So you have caught one today and Mr Edgeware had his yesterday. It only needs poor Mr Casini to have some success now," said McCallum benignly, as if he were personally responsible for the fair distribution of salmon among his guests.

"Ah," Marples laughed. "He gets out of it by saying it was his salmon rod which he lent Edgeware yesterday which caught the ten-pounder."

"Does he indeed?" Cliff thoughtfully left the bar. It had been a not unprofitable interlude after all.

15

ON HIS OWN suggestion, Casini accompanied Dempster and Tania to the platform yard at Strathcon the following morning. It would, he sensibly pointed out, save Tania coming all the way back to the hotel to pick him up, as the starting off point for their climb was some miles outside the village on the south road.

At Strathcon Tania introduced the two men to the yard boss, Bill Wilkins. "We're just delivering Mr Spencer to you, Bill. I'm going back with Mr Casini. We have a date to climb Stob Dearg."

"Well take care of Tania, Mr Casini. Yon looks an evil hill to me."

"Don't worry, Mr Wilkins. It's safer than your dock."

"Dinna ye believe it, mon."

Bill Wilkins was a stocky man with a slight stoop. He wore the traditional yard bowler hat, a relic of his Clydeside origins, where he had learned to build the best ships in the world. Now, at fifty-four, he had turned his hand to the second of two platforms to be built for Consolidated Oil. By this time Bill was an extremely wealthy man. He still owned shares in a Clydebank yard and was sole owner of the graving dock which proclaimed itself Wilkins Fabrications Ltd in large capitals.

The huge 20,000-ton platform lay on its side, four prodigious legs protruding. Once upended on the ocean bed, its superstructure would be added to give a final height of 700 feet above the sea floor. The four of them paused, admiring it.

"When that gets going there'll be thirty different shafts operating." Wilkins beamed affectionately at his monster, the lines on his face multiplying like crumpled parchment. "I subcontract much o' the work here, Meester Spencer," he explained to Cliff. "It saves a lot o' labour problems. Consolidated Oil have invested a few million pounds in this hunk o' steel, as ye probably know, and they've gone into the floating ones as well."

"Where's this one going?" Cliff asked.

"This yin's going to the Thule field. It'll be towed out on that big flotation collar ye can see underneath, that tubular thing. It's its life-jacket, ye see."

"How is it anchored to the ocean floor?" Casini wanted to know.

"Through its boots," Wilkins smiled. "Jist like tent pegs, and we've got the biggest pile driver in the world for a mallet. Do you realise that on Consolidated Oil Platform Two — the one you see here — more steel has been used than on the Forth Bridge? Aye, it's mind blowing, as they say nowadays."

"It's certainly an enfant terrible, Bill." Tania gazed at it dubiously. "But I have misgivings about the creation of such monsters."

"Och, you're too much of a back-to-nature, girl, Tania," Wilkins teased affectionately. "We've got to compromise, you know. People must live, and we need oil…"

"Oh, yes, I know all the arguments. I'm not really blaming you. We're all equally involved. It just doesn't seem right in this Highland setting though, does it?"

"Well, d'ye ken, Tania, I'm inclined to agree with you. But don't tell my workers. It's called progress."

Tania looked at her watch. "Goodness, we'll have to dash, Emile, won't we? I'll be back as soon as I'm off the hill, Hugh. Will that be all right?"

"Sure." Dempster agreed easily. "Don't fall off or — er, anything," he added, catching her eye, teasingly.

"She will be, how do you say, in good hands," Casini drawled.

So it was agreed that Cliff would have lunch with Bill Wilkins who promised to run him back to Inverloch if Tania and Casini looked like being late. As the dust settled behind the Lotus Mini, Cliff turned his gaze to the platform, and took some shots with his Rollei 35.

"How long does it take to get it sited, Bill?"

"About forty days, give or take a couple. It takes three days to flood the graving dock alone. That's after the gates themselves have the water in them pumped oot. Then they're towed away. The really awkward part is tilting the whole shooting match when it's been towed out to the site." His pale blue eyes seemed to be visualising the scene which was to take place in a week or so, as he gazed out to the tightly stretched line of the sea beyond. "It must go down the right way up, exactly on target. There's a crucial period of aboot three minutes when the whole caboodle is shifted from the horizontal to forty-five degrees. That's done by flooding the flotation collar, but it's no' my job, thank goodness. We just make the brutes. The American technicians do the positioning."

"Would you mind if I studied the platform more closely and got some pictures?"

"Not at all, lad, not at all. You'll find Callum Sinclair or Duncan Grant over there if you want any more information. Callum's in the wee yellow cabin."

"Thanks, Bill. I'll see you later then."

"Fine," he replied. "I'll leave you to your own devices. When you want to see me, just come over to my office — it's close to the main gate. And I might persuade you to a wee dram before we lunch. It's a snell wind here on the coast, and I always have a bottle handy: for medicinal purposes, ye ken!"

Cliff meandered over towards the network of tubes which formed the platform. He felt crowded by the immensity of it all — as if he was shrinking in his shoes. He passed two revolver cranes which worked in tandem, each capable of lifting 800 tons. The flotation collar towered above him as he walked along the base, a raft of 10,000 tons; high in the air, attached to the other two 'sleeping' horizontal legs, were the spherical flotation spheres: each 560 tons. They would prevent the whole platform from turning turtle when the flotation raft was flooded out at the site. They would gradually fill with water and allow the platform to find its sea legs on the ocean floor. Cliff continued along the curve of the huge cylindrical float. There was the constant din of a shipyard. Most of the workmen were on the other side of the platform, where the cranes worked like Siamese twins, lifting a long tubular member onto the lower part of the frame. To his right, another crane — a high jib Manitowoc — was resting easily on its wide tracks, the operator reading a newspaper in the cab. Soon Dempster reached the point where the flotation raft angled into the platform — the raft consisting of two interconnected tuning-fork shaped units on which the platform rested.

Quite suddenly there was complete and utter blackness. The roar of the machinery was superceded by a much more immediate roaring inside his skull. Bolts from the small sack which had knocked him out spilled across the ground as it fell. Two workmen — dark hair showing beneath their white hard hats — grabbed Dempster and dragged him towards a large steel bucket about six feet high, to which the crane cable was attached. It was on the side facing the platform, out of sight. They heaved him into the bucket and he toppled over the side, head first, fortunately saved from greater injury by a coil of dirty rope lying in the bottom of the bucket. The whole operation was completed within seconds in the privacy of the recess. The workmen climbed into the bucket beside him; then one gave a loud whistle. The crane driver looked up...

The bucket rose smoothly for 250 feet until it was suspended above the flotation sphere. With hand signals, one of the men guided it until it was just touching the top of the sphere; in its present reclining position this, with a corresponding partner on the other leg, was the highest point on the platform. The unconscious Dempster was lifted out of the bucket, none too gently, and dropped through a manhole in the plating of the sphere. It is probable that he would have been killed, if he'd fallen to the bottom, as the float was over fifty feet in diameter, but reinforcing struts, six feet below, broke his fall, and he lay draped on his stomach across a latticework of square tubing. The two workmen stared down at him; one gave a short laugh as he turned away. One oval dished steel manhole cover was

131

levered into position over the hole. It located accurately over twenty-two studs spaced round the perimeter. With ratchet spanners they tightened it in place. They clambered from the sphere to the platform down steel rungs, and ran out welding cable from a heavy mounted drum on a catwalk. While one climbed back onto the sphere, the other handed equipment up to him. It was a completely silent operation. They started to weld the manhole in place with heavy mild steel rods. Working clockwise on opposite sides, when they had made a complete run, they worked back in the opposite direction. It took over twenty minutes to fill the groove with runs of welding.

It might have been called a neat piece of workmanship.

16

DEMPSTER CAME TO again, more than an hour after he had been slugged. He was draped over the tubing, camera dangling under his face with the strap caught under his chin. The lower part of his chest felt as if it had been massaged by a tank. Sensing a drop below him, he spat. There was a drop. It was pitch black, and some distance to the floor of his prison, he realised. What had happened? Where was he? Painfully, he tried to remember and his mind gradually clarified. Who the hell had hit him? He had been standing beside the flotation collar when it happened. Someone must have been lurking in the shadows. He gave an experimental call and was jeered at by his own voice: hollow, metallic.

"Come on, you idiot, Dempster — sorry, Spencer — snap out of it!"

He heaved himself up and turned so that he was sitting astride the tube, then started to ease himself along in the direction from which he felt a stream of fresh air. He was thwarted by a wall: a wall of solid steel. It seemed to be curved. Yes, it was like the inside of a globe; that accounted for the weird acoustics: a sphere of sheet steel. He called again. Irrelevantly he wondered if this could be the ultimate in hi-fi? Sitting inside your own loudspeaker — it could even be transparent! He had no doubt as to which sphere he was trapped inside; it was the one on the very top of the ruddy platform — the one which would be filled with water when they laid the platform down on the ocean floor. He

133

was going to snuff it in style, he told himself. If he didn't die from starvation, he'd be drowned when they flooded the bloody thing. Flooded...there must be a valve somewhere: that breath of fresh air. His hands explored with the sensitive touch of a blind man, and found a hole. Then disappointment surged through him. It was only about four inches in diameter, and extended outwards a foot. A valve, obviously, but only of service to an emaciated rabbit.

The air in the sphere was stuffy. It smelt of welding flux and an anti-corrosive, which added up to one hell of a stink. He decided to climb up. There might possibly be a trapdoor. The effort made him feel as weak as if someone had sucked the marrow from his bones. He found a built-in steel ladder. A few minutes later there was cold blank steel above his head. He explored with one hand and found a slight recess. It was still warm. He could feel the edge of the plate where the welding had been done. Bastards! Then he moved back down to his perch. How long could a man live without water, he pondered, and what was the cubic capacity of a sixteen-metre sphere? There seemed to be enough air coming through that hole. But what did it matter? What did anything matter? Swartze would piss himself laughing if he could see me now, he thought bitterly. Not so ruddy efficient after all, are you, Mr Dempster?

"Hello, is that you, Callum?"

"Aye,"

"Bill here. Have you seen that big chap from Consolidated Oil?"

"He passed by a few hours ago," the site manager replied. "Why, what's up?"

"He should have come back by now. I was going to take him to the Strathcon Hotel for lunch."

"Well, if I see him, I'll tell him."

"Thanks."

Bill waited until 1.30 and decided to go down to the works canteen for a bite on his own, and left a message in his office. By 3 pm he was distinctly worried. He'd been working on the

134

details of another big contract, but his mind wasn't on it. Slightly irritated, he picked up the phone again.

"Callum?"

"Yes."

"Ask around and find out if this bloke — Spencer — has been seen. He seems to have vanished. I checked up at the gate a wee while ago. He hasn't left the place."

It was almost two hours later when Tania's call came through to Bill.

"Oh, hello there, Tania. Had a good day?"

"Just got back, Bill. It was super, but took us longer than we thought. I assumed Hugh Spencer would be back by now, but I haven't seen him in the Hotel." There was a longish pause. "Are you still there, Bill?"

"Yes, I'm here, Tania... Perhaps you'd better come over." Bill spoke slowly. "Meester Spencer has apparently disappeared."

"What?" Tania's voice was sharp. "He couldn't have done! He was just going to look at the platform — I can't understand it."

"Aye, well, that may be, Tania. But he never turned up for lunch; I've had a discreet but thorough search made and there's no sign of him."

"I'm coming over, Bill," she said.

A late shift was working but, as it was after normal working hours, the main entrance of the Dock was closed. Tania gave her name and the security guard opened the gate. Bill's office was just inside, and she saw a beat-up old Ford, with cauliflower wings, standing outside. Bill was not out to impress people with the baubles of success. There was another man in the office with him, and they were both studying some drawings on a wide cluttered desk.

"Oh, Tania. Good to see you — sit you down. Still no word, I'm afraid... This is Callum Sinclair — been with me since we were rivet boys in the dark days."

"Hello, Callum."

"Guid ti meet yi, Miss Olsen." A large rambling man touched his cap. His hands were calloused and he had the black-jowled

135

face of a two-shave-a-day man who didn't often make it.

"Callum made most of the enquiries about Mr Spencer," Bill explained. "We just canna understand it. He seems to have vanished. We've come to the conclusion that he can't have left the dock area by any normal means. Believe it or not, our man at the gate knows everyone of the two thousand workmen on the site... Jock Milne's an ex-policeman and has a fantastic memory. He's quite positive that Spencer didn't pass through the main gates. Now, all the other gates are kept locked for security reasons. We've looked in all the likely places where there might have been an accident — and drawn a blank..."

"Aye, and there are plenty o' them," Callum put in. "Though we've an amazing history o' safety on this job." Callum's look dared her to disagree, and he continued, "The oil platform companies have evolved a very thorough safety programme — in conjunction with the unions, of course..." An ardent fervour glinted in his small, dark eyes. It was obvious in which direction Callum's political leanings lay. "The Graythorp Safety Manual was the result o' that. But all the same," he conceded, "accidents can happen anywhere..."

"Would you care for a dram, or a cup of tea?" Bill tried to ease the tension.

"No thanks, Bill."

"Well, I don't know what to do, really," Bill said uncertainly, stroking his hair. "I think we've done all we can here, don't you, Callum?"

"Aye," the prickly Callum looked directly at Tania. "Do you have any idea what might have happened to him, Miss Olsen? Or what he was particularly interested in?"

"No, I'm as much in the dark as either of you."

There was a knock on the office door and an enormous man wearing a bowler looked in.

"Ah didna know ye had a veesitor," he announced.

"Come in, Duncan," Bill said warmly, "You just knocking off?"

"Aye, I am, and a bit late at that," the man replied. Duncan Grant had spent most of his life in Clydeside yards and had known both Bill and Callum for over thirty years. He had moved up north with Bill when he started the Strathcon dock. He was site overseer. He smiled at Tania when Bill introduced them, and then took off his bowler hat to reveal a head completely devoid of hair. He dropped the hat on the drawing board alongside Callum. It gave a dull thud. Callum caught Tania's look of surprise.

"Aye, the bowler was the traditional bonnet o' the yaird foremen, miss. Duncan's here is jest a helmet in disguise, to keep up with the tradeetions, ye ken."

"Well I remember the time when an unpopular foreman had a saer heed from someone dropping a rivet or bolt on him," Duncan reminisced.

"No sign o' Meester Spencer, Duncan?"

"Nae," the big man echoed, his huge frame giving a heave. "Nae hide or hair o' him. He was seen by some o' the boys this mornin' on the far side o' the platform, but neething mair... I didna like to ask too many o' the men," Duncan elaborated, "but the man jest seems tae have disappeared!"

"Aye, it's a bloody mystery," Bill echoed, "if Tania will forgive my language."

"The ither reason I came in Callum, was aboot those tallies." Duncan stated hitching a massive thumb into his belt. Round the trousers of his baggy pin stripe suit his belt looked a memento of less prosperous times, black with age and the buckle protesting at the last hole.

"Whit aboot them?"

"He means the Italian workmen," Bill explained to Tania.

"Aye, they've been using the crane bucket instead o' the lift," Duncan spat out. "They're too bloody lazy to walk ower to the bottom o' it! An, furthermore, they sealed over that flotation sphere an' I was wanting to have a look at it tomorrow."

"That's the one that was treated wi' the anti-corrosive a day or so back?" Bill asked.

"Aye that's it."

"I'll hae a word wi' all the crane drivers the mornin', Duncan. They were told already not to take anybody up wi' the cranes. It's agin the rules. My, they're bloody fools those icecream men

— they'd be cutting their own throats if they tried to claim insurance if they wir hurted."

"Will ye be needing any further help, then?" Duncan boomed. "A'm quite willing tae stay on if ye like."

"That's guid o' ye, Duncan, ye could be useful. I think we'll have tae have another wee look aboot before I contact the law. They'll have to be informed sooner or later," he turned gently to Tania.

"A-richt then, I'll jist ring the missus, so she willna dry up ma dinner." Duncan's enormous fingers were not designed for telephone dials, and he automatically produced a ballpoint from his breast pocket to dial with.

"That pen — " Tania arrested his hand, eagerly. It was just a cheap biro, but had an unusual snake design on the clip.

"It's surely no yours, Miss Olsen," Duncan started. "I found it beside the platform just now."

"Where? Can you remember where?"

"On the far side, under the flotation collar, it was."

"Can we go down there, please," she turned to Bill.

"Aye, lassie, but what's the matter, ye're behaving as if ye just found the Holy Grail or something."

"I've just found Hugh Speencer's pen. Or rather Mr Grant has." She looked eagerly at the yard owner.

"Let's go," he said. "Give Tania a helmet, Callum. I forgot to give one to Spencer this morning."

They all squeezed into Bill's old car. When Duncan got in the front it gave a lurch and stayed with a list for the short journey to the platform.

"On the far side, Bill, by the high jib Manitowoc," the big man directed.

As they walked over towards the platform Bill tried to lighten the tense silence. "Did you know, Tania, one o' those cranes doon at the bottom end o' the platform can lift eighty double-decker buses at one go..."

"Why should you want to do that, Bill?" Tania asked.

"Oh, jest a press hand-oot, lassie, ye ken. It is supposed to impress."

"I am impressed without any statistics, Bill."

138

"Where was the place ye found that biro, Duncan?" Bill addressed the big man. Duncan looked round.

"Over there," he pointed to the side of the flotation collar, beside the crane bucket.

"There don't seem to be many men working tonight, Bill," Tania ventured looking about.

"No, the holidays are upon us, lass, but we have a full complement on the day shift and anyway, most o' the late shift are working over on the other side this evening."

They stopped beside the flotation collar.

"It was jest right here." Duncan kicked his toe around in some small bolts which lay scattered in the dust.

"I suppose it has been searched under the collar?" Bill asked Callum.

"Of course man, whit di ye take me for?" He glowered at his friend as if his very integrity had been doubted.

"Dinna, fret, Callum, a' was only askin'."

"I've looked everywhere humanly and inhumanly possible."

Tania was gazing up at the huge framework above. She steadied herself by holding onto the side of the heavy steel bucket. Suddenly she exclaimed, "The bucket, Bill, he could have gone up in the bucket."

"Not a chance lassie," Callum replied abruptly. "The crane drivers may bend the rules to take the workmen up, but never a stranger."

"Callum's right, Tania," Bill looked at her with sympathy. "They'd never take up someone from outside."

"They'll never take up a workman agin if I catch them either," Duncan growled.

"I suppose we should go up top and have a look round anyhow," Bill suggested. "If Meester Spencer didn't drop the biro doon here, then it could have fallen from up above."

"Weel, I suppose so," Callum grudgingly admitted, "but we were all over the platform earlier."

They moved along to the cage lift, and shot up instantly. When Bill opened the door Tania was amazed to realise that they had stopped. Leading from the elevator ahead of them, was a naked steel catwalk. It followed the top of the south upper leg, revealing a dizzy drop to the ground far below. Only a thin handrail either side offered any sense of security.

Callum led the way, striding confidently along the Expandamet decking. The others followed silently. The noise became more intense as they passed the halfway point. Riveters were working on the far side of the platform.

Tania could see Bill's car far below, beside the edge of the torpedo-shaped float.

"I hope you've got a good head for heights, Tania," Bill remarked.

"Bit late to ask her now," Duncan laughed. "We're halfway there."

"I'm fine, Bill. Heights don't bother me much, though your car seems to have shrunk a bit!"

Callum had now reached the first of the pile guides.

"The piles that go through these guides are over fifty inches in diameter," Bill commented as he waited for her to go through ahead of him. He stooped as he went through the 'eye' of the guide. "Forty-four of them hold the auld dear on the bottom," he added affectionately.

"It's difficult to imagine," Tania replied, zipping up her anorak against the biting wind. They arrived safely on the far side of the guide, on the continuation of the catwalk. Callum's voice floated back.

"The crane wire gives a good plumb line to where Duncan found the pen."

Tania glanced upwards to the jib to where the steel wire came over a sheave.

To her left was one of the two flotation spheres.

"You would have trouble hiding a speugy here never mind someone as big as Meester Spencer," Bill commented. They had all stopped and were looking down to the ground.

"Weel, I did say," Callum warned, "we'd have seen him had he been up here." His tone indicated that they were wasting time.

Tania looked at Duncan Grant. "Mr Grant, you mentioned some, how do you call them, 'tallies' were working on one of these spheres weren't they?"

"Aye that's right. This one here," he gave the huge steel football a thump with his outstretched hand.

"He," she started nervously, "he, just couldn't be inside could he?"

"Dinna be daft lassie," Duncan broke out with a laugh. How on earth could he get inside the thing?"

Bill looked at her curiously. "What makes you suggest that Tania?" he asked gently.

"I don't know. It's just that...well he must be somewhere."

Callum had taken up a bolt which was on a wire basket attached to the catwalk and gave the side of the sphere a series of rapid blows. He then put his ear to the metal. Tania did the same.

There seemed to be a pause, even in the riveting on the other side of the structure. Then Tania's face lit up and she whirled round to Bill Wilkins. "He's *there* Bill, he's *inside*."

"She's right, Bill," Callum confirmed slowly." It's either him or the ghost of a woodpecker..."

17

"HE'S SEALED IN, then?" Duncan's voice was low and hard. "The puir bugger's welded in."

"We'll have to burn him out," Bill stated. Once convinced of the situation he proved a man of action. "Start running oot the burner hoses from the pig socket back there, Callum, will you? Give him a hand, Duncan. And Tania?"

"Yes?"

"Would you go back to the cage. You'll see a length of rope on the RSJ beside it. Can you bring it along?"

"Okay, Callum. But what's an RSJ?"

"A Rolled Steel Joint: a girder, in your language."

"Right," Tania's voice held a note of relief. She was glad to have something positive to do and retraced her steps quickly. Glancing back, she saw Bill silhouetted against the evening sky. Behind him, a white plastic sheet, bearing the large letters CO, was draped round the sphere. Callum soon returned, assisted by Duncan. The latter was heaving lengths of twin hosing which hung down below the catwalk. They were connected to a central oxygen and propane supply. He handed the burner to Duncan who glanced at the nozzle:

"Aye, it's a standard nozzle, but it'll do."

"It's completely welded up then?" Bill asked the rugged Glaswegian. Duncan grimaced, glancing sideways at the steel ball as he climbed up the rungs.

142

"Like a maximum security prison. Don't know how he's still alive!"

"Aye, it's a fifty-foot fall inside…"

"He must have caught up on one of the cross members," Callum paused for an instant. "Otherwise, he'd have broken his neck."

"Perhaps he has?"

"We'll soon find out, but he's still alive anyway."

"Can you pass that lot up, Bill?"

"Hold on, I'll move up a couple of rungs."

"There… Got it?" Duncan grunted and moved back up, powerful muscles bulging in his upper arm as he hauled himself upwards.

"That's enough," Duncan's voice floated down.

"I'll come up now," Callum told him. By the time he arrived, Duncan had turned the burner on and was just pulling on a pair of goggles. A moment later, a stream of molten metal cascaded down the side of the sphere. Bill watched it and prayed fervently that none of it would be hot enough to set his car on fire — it was directly below the operation.

"Hey, Bill."

"Yes?"

"Can you get an air line as well? We're frightened we may fry Mr Spencer, if he has to come through this hole. It'll cook him rarely, there's so much metal heated up now."

"Okay, give me a couple of minutes."

Tania came back along the catwalk, with the coil of Corlene rope tucked under her arm.

"You going home, Bill?"

"No such luck, Tania. I'm the errand boy for the two gaffers up on the sphere. They want air now."

"I thought there was all the air from here to Canada blowing over just now," she shivered. "It might almost be winter!"

"Aye, it gets a bit perky at night sometimes… No, they need an air line for cooling off the hole. I think they'll have him out soon."

"Thank goodness," she breathed. Glancing up, she saw that the molten metal was now being blown into the sphere; Duncan

143

was angling it to one side to localise this danger. He only hoped that Cliff was not immobile and in direct line of fire.

"Would you turn this valve on when Callum gives the word? I'll take the rope."

"What are they doing exactly?" Tania enquired.

"Cutting oot a new trapdoor for Mr Spencer on the top o' the sphere."

Bill went back along to the rungs. "Are ye there," he shouted.

Callum's head appeared over the curve of metal. "Okay, Bill, pass up that rope and the hose. We'll have the hole done in a couple o' shakes." He reached down a hand to his friend. "Duncan's cut the circle round one o' the rungs, so that we can lower it down inside."

"Aye," Bill acknowledged. "Tania will turn on the air."

"Thanks."

"Jist aboot roon, Callum," Duncan called. He could feel his legs smarting from spark burns.

"She's starting to swing."

Callum threaded the double rope through the rung and tied it. He then put a turn of rope round a lower rung and said, "I can hold it now."

"That's it then." There was an ugly grinding noise as the heavy section of metal broke away, stuck an instant, then dropped. It was stopped short by the rope with a jerk. Duncan turned the burner off, dropped it and grabbed the rope to help Callum.

"Okay, Callum, I have it." They eased it down gently, the friction taken up round the rung in place beside them.

They heard a clanging noise.

"The cross ribbing," Callum explained, as Duncan paused. Eventually a deeper note indicated that it had reached the bottom.

Duncan peered down into the hole whilst Callum played air over the freshly cut edge.

"Are you all right, Meester Spencer?"

"Yes, I'm fine, but I feel like a lonely sardine."

"You're not injured then?" Callum now shouted.

"Just a few bruises."

"Is he all right?" Tania appeared beside them. Callum turned in surprise.

"You shouldn't have come up here miss. It's no place for a girl."

"Is he all right?" she repeated impatiently.

"Aye he's fine," Duncan replied. Bill joined them at that moment.

"You dashed up there as if you spent all your spare time on the Eiffel Tower."

"I've just been telling her off, Bill."

"She's probably safer than we are," Bill chuckled. "I hear the big lad's okay?"

"He's just coming up."

Dempster's head appeared at the hole. Duncan reached down and grasped him by the shoulders and, despite his size, lifted him out as if he was a sack of waste paper.

"Well that's better," Cliff exclaimed, brushing down his clothes which were stained with red lead, "I must thank you folks."

"Are you sure you're not hurt?" Tania was still anxious.

"No, I'm fine." He glanced questioningly at Callum and Duncan.

"I'm Callum Sinclair; I saw you go by my office today." He jerked a thumb at Duncan. "And this is Duncan Grant, who used the tin-opener..."

"How on earth did you get inside it?" Bill asked, his knuckles white on the rungs.

"I thought it would be a good viewpoint for some photographs." Cliff's expression was studiedly apologetic. "The lid was off the thing, and I must have moved slightly as I was looking through the viewfinder — I don't remember anything else. I guess I fell through the hole and was then sealed in somehow or other. I must have been unconscious for a bit... It's entirely my own fault," he ended lamely.

"You've got to thank Tania for finding you, Mr Spencer. It was her idea that you might be in the sphere."

"Yes, she's more than just a beautiful face," Cliff acknowledged, as they explained how they had found him. "Tania has the gift of second sight. Her mother was a white witch."

145

"Weel, let's get off this bloody catwalk before we enter my car by the sun roof!" Bill said, leading the way back to the lift cage.

"I'm afraid I smell a bit like a painter," Dempster apologised.

"I smell something fishy about the whole bleeding business, Mr Spencer." Bill screwed up his small eyes, as he looked at Cliff. "But we'll find the culprits, have no doubt."

Callum broke the uncomfortable silence. "If you've had a crack bad enough to knock ye oot, Mr Spencer, you should see the doctor."

"Not me. I know what would happen, whisked inside for observation. No, I'll get back to the hotel and have a slap-up feed. There's still time, I think." He glanced at his watch. "Can I invite you good people as well?"

"Naw laddie, we've got ti get back. There's a hard day ahead tomorrow, an' I canna abide that McCallum, he's like a flounder," Bill said. Tania gave a laugh, the nervous tension in her had been released.

"Well what did you find out about friend Casini?" Dempster asked as they drove back to the hotel in the Mini.

"Not much. He's quite close about his personal activities; but I would think given half a chance his activities could be very personal as far as I'm concerned..."

"Did he *get* half a chance?"

Tania gave an amused chuckle and shook her head. "We kept moving all day."

"No hint of what he's really doing up here?"

"Not a thing. As soon as I steered the conversation to his work or himself, he carefully turned it back into safer channels."

"Did you do any rock climbing?"

"Just a scramble, as he called it, but it was a superb view from the summit, at least it was a better view than you had."

He grinned. They were silent for a moment, then Tania said, "You know I don't believe a word about you stepping backwards with your camera. And I don't think Bill Wilkins does either. Are you going to tell me what really happened?"

Between them they pieced together the likely course of events.

"It was some Italian workmen that welded the manhole in place," Tania told him.

"Yes, and a possible connection there with Casini. The tentacles of the Mafiosa Sicilia are long."

"The crane driver must have been in on it as well."

"I suppose so. There's been quite a bit of infiltration of baddies into the oil business these past few years." He turned to her abruptly. "Tania, I don't think you should go out with Casini again."

"Jealous?"

"Not exactly. If he's just had a go at eliminating me — you could be next!"

"But why?"

"Yes, why, that's the question... I think I'm beginning to see a light. I told you Alasdair and I went out to have a look at the Point House, didn't I? Well we had an observer when we came away and I think that observer was Casini. He would know I was snooping after something. If he's the pro I think he is, he probably also knows I've frisked his room."

"Well he was in a very relaxed mood today, really carefree."

"He probably thought he was free of me — for good!"

"You think he knows what your real connection is with Consolidated Oil, then?"

"I guess so. I'm afraid your boss has made a balls up of my cover. I should have arranged it myself."

"Mr Swartze likes 'overthinking' things," Tania murmured.

"Huh. But do you realise what the really interesting thing is? The Laird's dead. Wilson's job is more or less done if we can believe the implications of that letter. There should be no trouble now in getting James McBride to sell. It's only a matter of to which company, and Wilson has the necessary pressure to apply. So why, I ask myself, does somebody — Casini or whoever — feel obliged to wipe me out? What has he got to be afraid of me finding out?"

"I see what you mean."

"It's the sixty-four-thousand-dollar question, isn't it?"

18

A MURKY CLOUD ceiling descended at dusk. Shadows linked hands, advancing from their moorland homes. The air was still. Dempster left the hotel by a rear exit, via the boiler room. He skirted south of the village and reached Alasdair's house through the small garden at the rear. He had phoned arranging to be there at 1.30 am and it was precisely 1.29 when he silently opened the back door and entered the house.

"Come on in, Cliff."

"You've got good ears, for a man of your age!"

Alasdair chuckled and put the light on.

"Didn't hear a thing — just know from old, if you said 1.30 you wouldn't be more than three seconds late, and I guessed you'd be about half a minute early."

"Yes, it's a dangerous thing to be predictable," Cliff agreed, sitting down. He noticed that Alasdair had put a piece of hardboard over the front of the window as well as drawing the blind.

"Are you fit enough for your breaking and entering act?"

"I feel fine. I had a bit of shut eye." He elaborated on the day's mishap.

"So you think that Casini may be behind this last episode?" Alasdair asked.

"That's right. He's got everything loaded in his favour and he's still a nervous man."

"We'd better find out why, then, hadn't we?"

"That's why I'd like to visit the boathouse again, and I'd like you to create a disturbance with the dory."

"So we take the boat?"

"Yes, we'll row round first and we can do the boathouse job. Then can you cause a diversion while I go through the house?"

"Right — I'm just an apprentice; but I'll do anything you say..."

"Thanks, Alasdair."

"Had any more thoughts about the Laird?"

"I've plenty of thoughts," Cliff answered seriously, looking at his watch. "Confirmation is what I'm after..."

"What was Wilson doing today?"

"Working in his lab — all day, I checked."

"The other guests at the hotel?"

"Fishing. Casini was off climbing with Tania on Stob Dearg. I gave the police a ring, by the way, and we have a meeting with an Inspector Galloway, tomorrow."

"Oh?"

"At the Benmore Junction Hotel."

"Yes, we will have a few things to discuss. Why the return visit to the Point House?"

Dempster didn't reply, but took a letter out of his pocket and passed it to his friend. It was the envelope which had arrived by Special Delivery earlier in the day. Alasdair read the contents carefully.

"So," he replied eventually, "it payed off to send the hand down to the boffins in the south, didn't it?"

"Seems like it," Cliff replied taking the letter again.

"That bit about the wool. I can hardly believe it?"

"Oh, it's right, that lab is not known for its mistakes."

"You'll be blinding the local Johns with science..."

The boat glided silently into a pocket in the rocks close to the boathouse. It had been a longer row than Cliff had anticipated. He jumped ashore and held the painter; Alasdair followed suit. Together they lifted the bow noiselessly up onto the rocks. Climbing the low cliff, they reached the boundary wall and paused there for a minute; then climbed over. Close to the boathouse, they stopped again, absorbed in the shadows of the bushes.

Cliff reached the back entrance to the boathouse and was soon inside, closing the door behind him. He made a cursory inspection of the interior before going over to the launch. He didn't bother examining the wheelhouse, but made straight for the padlocked hold which once again did not detain him unduly. His torch located the canvas stowage sacks where he had last seen them. This time he inspected the dry suit meticulously. A small tear caught his attention and a tiny object. Dempster paused and smiled in the darkness. He locked up the hold, then went to the stern of the launch and lowered himself into the large rubber boat tied to the stanchion. He gave this his undivided attention for a further ten minutes, before rejoining his companion.

"Right. Back to the dory," he murmured to Alasdair. "Give me about five minutes, then start her up, away from the boathouse."

"It'll take me about that time to get out there," Alasdair whispered his reply. "Good luck — see you back at Tigh Bhan."

The house lay in total darkness, a sullen white hulk. The note of the outboard starting up shattered the still night. The motor eased off as the boat came closer in, and Cliff saw a chink of light in an upstairs window, a tiny crack at the edge of a blind. Then he heard a faint grating noise as the front door opened. From his viewpoint, he could see both the front entrance, where the steps met the gravel, and the whole of the back door. He moved towards the latter as soon as two shadowy figures were visible against the few stars in that northern sky. Predictably, he encountered a standard three lever lock which took a minute and a half to open. Then he moved into a darkened hallway which led to stairs directly ahead; on each side was a passageway — he presumed that one led to the rooms on the west side of the house, probably the front door as well; the other to the kitchen, ʲining room, and toilet.

Out at sea, the noise of the outboard died away. Cliff moved lently on up the stairs; a dim, rather eerie light was cast from a ⁾loured glass roof light in the stair well. There were two storeys. He paused on the first landing, where a window in front of him overlooked the sea to the north. He studied the ground below and fancied he could see two faint outlines by the rhododendrons; one appeared to be holding a small telescope to his eye: a night viewer, he realised; they seemed to have quite a collection of toys. A ghostly shadow, far over the water, betrayed the whereabouts of Alasdair's dory. He smiled grimly, and turned to the room on his right, but the mere fact that the blind was not drawn made him dismiss it. He decided that the occupants probably slept in the top rooms and, moreover, in one of them Stewart's wife would be waiting for her husband to return! He would have to trust to luck, he decided. He couldn't wait indefinitely outside a door, listening for a tell-tale yawn.

The next room he entered was in complete darkness. He closed the door and rapidly examined it by the light of his torch. Clothing was scattered on the chairs, the bed, and about the floor. The bed was obviously in use — blankets strewn about, as if its owner had departed in haste. On its far side he found what he wanted: a filthy black pullover. He sniffed at it — garlic, oil, and also some other kind of oil... Lanoline? he asked himself, looking with distaste at the huge garment. It could only belong to one person. He broke off a loose strand of wool and put it in his pocket. A dirty shirt and stained white trousers, along with a pair of sea boots, lay heaped in one corner, beside a canvas sack similar to those in the hold of the boat. Some unwashed cups sat on the mantelpiece, and half-eaten food lay on a plate.

As Cliff closed the door behind him, he heard an engine's note rise. Alasdair was keeping them guessing. Five minutes later, he gained the cover of the three stately Wellingtonia and made his way circumspectly back to the boundary wall.

As he opened the back door of Tigh Bhan, the savoury smell of ground coffee brewing assailed his nostrils. He walked in, closed the door, and Alasdair switched on the light.

"Have a good picking?"

"Yes, I think so," he answered cheerfully, screwing up his eyes against the dazzling glare. "But they will have recognised you, Alasdair," he commented as he sat down. "The big lad was using an image intensifier — the sort used for night rifle sights."

Despite the late hour, Alan McCallum, the owner of Stob Dearg Hotel, was still more or less in his dinner suit. He was in bed with Morag; his wife had left for Dingwall to visit her mother the previous day. It was Molly's evening off and the guests had kept him up, drinking, until a quarter to two. He had cursed them half-heartedly, torn between the lure of money and that of other pleasures. As he held Morag, he thought of graves.

19

THE OVERCAST WEATHER of the night proved a false alarm and
the day of the Laird's funeral turned out to be an excellent
one for tourists, midges and salmon who prefer to remain at lib-
erty.

Tania had been invited fishing by the triumvirate of Casini,
Marples and Edgeware, and had persuaded Dempster that it
would be a good opportunity to try and pump the remaining
two oilmen. After she departed in a competitive flurry of
blandishments from her escort party, Dempster had a busy
morning. He put through several phone calls to London. One of
these was to an agency that, for a price, could find out most
things about most people, and he wanted more information on
the Canadian pilot, Jack Bourne. He also took the Mini over to
the Western Atlantic and gave Jim Atkinson another envelope
for Inverness airport.

That done, he collected Alasdair and they drove to the
Benmore Junction Hotel.

Charlie Galloway had taken an immediate liking to his two
visitors, and what they had told him had been of considerable
interest. Charlie was generally reckoned a big man, but he felt
physically dwarfed by Cliff and Alasdair, as the three of them
sat hunched round a coffee table in the hotel lounge. He smiled.
"Aye, it was considerate of you gentlemen to call on me, and
what you've told me, I may say, goes a long way in confirming

my suspicions. I've a man up at Strathcon at the moment looking into yesterday's little incident, Mr Dempster."

"So you know my right name too, Inspector?"

"Aye, we know quite a bit," Charlie responded with a chuckle. "As they say, we're not so green as we're cabbage looking…"

"How did you find out about the platform yard 'accident', Inspector?" Alasdair asked.

"Oh, we have our contacts," Charlie responded smugly. "I can put my finger on every man in that yard that has ulterior motives for working there."

"That's good to know," Alasdair returned. "Changed days from when I was a nipper."

"Oil is making us all change our ways in these parts," Charlie confided, "be it for better or worse I dinna ken."

The funeral service for Hector McBride of McBride was held in the old family chapel in the grounds of the estate, not far from Rhuda House itself. The long-since deceased architect of this structure had obviously thought it fitting that the household should have to walk at least a few yards on the Sabbath to attend to their devotions. The chapel, like the house, was constructed of sandstone, and hadn't been used since the funeral of the Hon. Mrs McBride, eight years previously. It had suffered in consequence, although it had been hastily renovated for this sad occasion — the grass surrounds had been cut and the weeds in the gravel were newly beheaded. Topmost layers of dust on windows and pews had been wiped off with a deft flick of the duster. But the place was fully prepared to lapse back into slumber until the demise of the next McBride, thought Alec Dubh sourly; he had been engaged, albeit ungraciously, upon the enormous task of cleaning the chapel up.

A sizeable crowd of people gathered to pay homage to the late Laird. Most of the local crofting menfolk were there, and quite a few county people were in attendance, including the local MP who had known and liked McBride. He had been on holiday at his sister's estate, Clustolan, further inland. Mr Orr, the Chief Constable, stood beside him. Though McBride and his family were not 'regular', the Rev. Hamish McAlpine welcomed the business: the dead should not be denied a decent burial and the old boy had to be fittingly despatched to his last fishing ground where McAlpine felt certain he would be well contented, provided there were no tourists. The Reverend felt fully justified in taking advantage of this gathering to say a few more words than usual, for he knew that a fitting repast had been prepared in the Big House. There had always been plenty of refreshment — old Hector had not denied himself good brandy and malt — and Hamish McAlpine couldn't abide drink!

Hughie the Hearse reflected on McBride, reposed now in his oak coffin. It looked very nice; a beautiful sheen off that wood — but costly. He fingered the square key in his pocket which he had used to tighten the lid just a short while before. It was warm-looking, that oak, a comforting permanence about it. After the service Hector was carried by eight pall-bearers along a sunny pathway to the small graveyard. Old Archie stood to attention at the grave, his spade held like a rifle. He attempted to stand erect but found it almost impossible. His rheumatism was bothering him, and the two 'starter' drams which Agnes had given him didn't help... As the coffin was laid gently alongside the grave, Archie gave vent to a loud hiccup. A red flush spread over Hughie's powdered dome and he glared savagely at the offender. 'Old bugger,' he muttered to himself. 'Always spoiling the act.' The soporific monotone of the Benediction, as performed by the Rev. Hamish McAlpine, seemed, to each member of the congregation, to be directed specifically at himself, but it required a Herculean endeavour to remain awake. Jerking to attention, like a tired puppet, Archie suddenly realised that it was all over... Spitting loudly in his open palms, he set to work, filling the old Laird in with an energy belying his eighty-two years. As was customary, Hughie had enacted the 'dust to dust' passage by throwing a token shower of gravel into the hole. There had been no flowers. Stones thundered down haphazardly on top of the coffin. Hughie the Hearse's face turned an unbecoming shade of purple.

"I'm back, Cliff." With a cursory knock, Tania came bursting into Dempster's room.

"Have a good day's fishing?"

"Yes, and, believe it or not, I caught a salmon."

"If it's over ten pounds, it'll cost you a small fortune!"

"Oh," she laughed, brushing her hair back. "No danger of that — it was a tiddler — only eight pounds."

"Not a bad tiddler for your first go," he commented. "Did you manage to land any information from the character with the French polished head or him of the tartan long johns?"

"No, they didn't talk shop at all. That creep Marples kept asking me questions about Mr Spencer — I'm surprised he hasn't collared you yet. I gather he knew Sir Hubert. So be warned."

"Thanks for the tip-off. That's one quarter where I'm tender, and won't stand a lot of quizzing…"

Archie was paralytic. He slept as he always did after a celebration (an almost nightly occurrence) in his baggy yellow-stained tweed suit — he suffered from cystitis. He had been unceremoniously dumped in the Estate Land Rover and later removed to the bed in his cottage by Johnny Bhan, only a small degree less drunk than himself.

Hughie the Hearse had arrived home in a filthy temper. After his supper he sealed down the flap of a white business envelope and addressed it to Cuthbertson and Elliot, Solicitors, Mayfield Street, Inverness. Old Elliot wanted the funeral account promptly, to wind up the estate business under the old Laird. This suited Hughie — he had discovered that a dead man's inheritors were not always too ready with their payment; they tended to bury the bill with the deceased. He stuck a stamp on the envelope and placed it carefully on the mantelpiece in the small, bare room which served as an office.

Then he took off his jacket and retired into his snuggery above the funeral parlour, where a bottle of Glen Grant stood stiffly at attention, like a soldier on duty. He locked the door, decapitated the bottle with a deft anti-clockwise twist, and smacked his pale lips in anticipation. He passed swiftly into a world where corpses laughed and joked, whilst the vaults of his mind rang with the sweet note of running whisky — a swirling river on which coffins floated like varnished canoes.

Paul Wilson and Captain Craig joined Cliff and Tania for dinner that evening. Wilson had the next day free and was eager to fix up their climbing foursome with Casini.

"In my opinion," Captain Craig grinned blandly around him, "climbing is an occupation for the mentally deficient. But I can tell you one thing, there's been a big high sitting out over Rockall like a broody hen. So you couldn't ask for better weather."

"That's great," Wilson said, "because I was going to suggest we try for a sea stack. There's a good one nearby."

"You mean the Rhuda Stack?" Dempster asked.

"That's right. It's about three hundred feet, but a good route. Very Severe, and the rock's excellent."

In the lounge over coffee Marples and Edgeware quickly attached themselves to Tania and the talk was of fishing. As he feared, Cliff found himself button-holed by Marples.

"The delightful Tania told me about you, Hugh," he beamed over his port. "I used to know your uncle — Mother Hub, we used to call him — quite well, you know."

Fortunately Cliff was saved by Paul Wilson bringing over Casini to sort out the details of their proposed climb.

They were talking climbing harnesses. McCallum, hovering as ever, accepted one of Casini's Gitanes and offered to dig an account of the first ascent of Rhuda Stack out of an old climbing journal he claimed to be able to lay his hand on in the hotel's meagre library.

"And I'd like to collect some of my climbing gear from your store-room, if I may," Wilson put in.

"Aye, I think it's open, Mr Wilson," McCallum replied. "If not, Morag will soon give you the key." And he sidled discreetly away to find an ashtray. McCallum never refused a cigarette from anybody, but he was finding Gitanes a bit strong for his taste.

It was midnight when Dempster arrived at Alasdair's cottage.

"Oh, it's you, Cliff. I wasn't really expecting you tonight."

"Just thought I'd drop by for a chat."

"Come on in by the fire." There was a log fire burning in the grate and it transformed the room, radiating a homely glow. The only other illumination was from a small table lamp, made out of a glass float.

"It's nice and snug here, lad," said Cliff approvingly. "Simple, but effective…"

"Can I get you anything to drink?"

"A cup of coffee later on would be fine…"

"Have a pew."

"Thanks." They settled back in the comfort of the two old chairs; Alasdair threw another piece of driftwood onto the fire and it started to spark.

"That's the trouble with pine," he complained. "Give me silver birch any day."

"Can you come round to the Stack with the dory tomorrow, Alasdair?" Cliff outlined to him the plan for the ascent of the Old Man of Rhuda.

"You seem a mite worried about the whole thing," Alasdair stated, looking at his friend from under his blond eyebrows.

"Wouldn't you be? A couple of arch villains, and the ideal situation for doing a bit of dirty work on the side…"

"Why go?"

"Got to get to the bottom of things. I'm a hundred per cent sure that Casini is the motivator. I will have to get him to show his hand more."

"And Wilson?"

"It could be he's in it more than I expect, but he seems to be such an amateur — except at his job — he's no sluggard at that. No," Dempster deliberated, "I think Casini's our man."

"What about those other oilmen at the hotel."

"I had a check done on them, they seem in the clear, and Tania's given them the once over."

"Some men have all the luck. What time do you want me round at the Stack?"

"Half past five."

"Anything else?"

"Nope. Just one thing," Cliff looked at his friend in an abstract way, "what do you know about McCallum?"

"McCallum? He's been here for as long as I can remember. He was born at Dundonnell, not far from where I picked you up at Alex Campbell's. He's above board, I think, apart from being involved in buying poached venison once. He was unlucky enough to be caught: it was the 'Toad', one of our local poachers, who shopped him. By the way, I've been asking some of those night workers if they've seen anything."

"And?"

"Jimmie Crichton saw a black inflatable the night the Laird died, up the Bhan, but it was too dark to identify it, he says. There were two people aboard and it was being rowed; I saw him after we got back from our meeting with Galloway. Just a hunch I had..."

"Mmm, that's interesting... What was that?" he whispered suddenly. Alasdair looked up quickly; his head cocked to one side, his big fists clenched instinctively. He rose silently and put out the light; then stood by the door. He couldn't hear anything, but he could feel the draught coming round where the door jamb wasn't a perfect fit. Looking round, and seeing Dempster in the fire-light, he raised a warning finger. Cliff slid easily into an upright position.

Fascinated, in the firelight they watched the door knob turning slowly. There was no sound, but the door started to open. It opened outwards into the kitchenette. Alasdair lifted one leg and lashed out at the door. There was a splintering of wood as it swung back and an oath in the far room; Alasdair followed it and Cliff heard the thud of heavy blows. Alasdair shot back through the opening as if fired from a cannon, landing close to the window, a good ten feet away. An enormous hulk followed him through the door and Cliff knew it could only be one person: the Spaniard from the Point House. A smaller man — Stewart at a guess — came after; both were dressed for night prowling in dark trousers and fisherman's jerseys.

Dempster had blended into the shadows by the door leading

159

to the front porch. His foot lashed out as the Spaniard charged past him and caught the side of his neck with a horrible crunch. The man was knocked towards the fire, head first into the flames. Letting out a terrible scream, he writhed in agony, his hands covering his face.

The smaller man whipped up Alasdair's half empty whisky bottle from the table with the speed of a mongoose. Then he sprang at Dempster, swinging this newly acquired club. Cliff was anticipating a blow but was caught out when Stewart threw it on the downward stroke. It caught him on the right temple and the bottle shattered in potent smithereens. Cliff fell backwards, unconscious.

Meanwhile, Alasdair had revived. He saw Stewart about to boot Dempster, and threw himself forward desperately on the floor, feet first; in a quick movement he brought one foot up into the other man's crutch. The blow carried a lot of force and Stewart went backwards fast, crashing into the table and breaking one of the drop leaves. Crouched on all fours, Bernadino was watching the scene with tears running down his cheeks, his face badly burned. Alasdair grabbed an old curling stone which served as a doorstop. It had been quarried on the Ailsa Craig and used by his father, but not for the use he now put it to as he threw it at the Spaniard. Had it found its mark, it would undoubtedly have killed him. But even in his present state, the big Spaniard's reactions were swift, and he dived forwards as the lump of polished granite smashed destructively into the tile fireplace. His out-stretched hands wrapped themselves round Alasdair's ankles. Unable to escape this vice-like grip, Alasdair found himself rising, all fourteen stones of him, and his head crashed through the old three-quarter-inch tongue and groove of the attic floor, between the joists, as though it was cardboard. He lost consciousness and fell to the floor.

Dempster came to in time to witness the final act of this drama. Casting around for a weapon his eye fastened on the CO_2 gun. A little present from A.J., he thought grimly, as he dropped an arrow into it and squeezed the trigger. There was a plop — as though a bottle of wine had been broached — and he saw that the arrow protruded from Bernadino's shoulder. From the bellow that issued from the huge man's scarred mouth, Cliff was very nearly satisfied that the shoulder joint was shattered. But out of the corner of his eye he noted warily that Stewart was back in circulation. A classic example of Glaswegian thuggery, he held the broken whisky bottle raised in his hand.

Suddenly there was a loud hammering on the door and PC Mackay's voice boomed: "Police. Open up there!"

Bernadino and Stewart spun round and were out of the back door in an instant. Cliff staggered out and opened the front door. "What's going on?" Trigger's voice held a sharp edge.

"Come in, Constable. Your timing was providential... Mr MacAlasdair and I were just having a work-out; I think we've had enough for tonight, don't you, Alasdair?" Cliff led the way inside, turning on the light. Trigger's eyes roamed round the room in disbelief.

"A work-out, did you say? It looks as if the house is being demolished! Just as well I was passing to drop in on the friendly party then!" Trigger was justifiably annoyed: the two men were having him on and he didn't like being made a fool of. "There've been a lot of funny goings on here lately... You may not have heard the last of this yet, Alasdair. There's such a thing as breach of the peace."

Alasdair was still dazed, sitting on the floor with blood streaming from splinters in his head. Trigger stared at him, and suddenly became aware of the hole between the beams.

"I just don't believe it, Alasdair. Your head made that hole?"

"Oh yes it did, Trigger. It really did. I was kind of helped up by the ankles. I would offer you a dram, but somehow or other the bottle fell off the table... Have you met Mr Spencer, Trigger? He's an oil man."

"Aye, I've seen him. Do you want to prefer charges against him?"

20

"WHAT ON EARTH happened to you?" Tania gazed in astonishment at the ugly blue swelling on Cliff's forehead. She had just joined him for breakfast.

"We had a reception at Alasdair's late last night," he explained softly. "Quite a riotous party, actually. A beat group from the Point House came over on a social call." Tania's eyes opened wider as she sat down. "Officially, I had a few whiskies last night, which I'm not used to, and slipped in the bathroom. I've already offered that explanation to McCallum and Casini." Tania glanced over at the Sicilian who sat by himself at a small table under a large water colour of Stac Polly.

"And the beat group, as you call them?"

"The big lad will be more sorry for himself than either Alasdair or I." Cliff's voice held a grim satisfaction, as he bit into a slice of buttered toast.

"How's Alasdair?" she enquired.

"Nothing that Rentokil won't cure. He went off to the local ju-ju man to get de-splintered after fielding some chunks of wood in his skull. Luckily, it wasn't some more vulnerable point."

"You're a callous brute," she remarked. "Sounds as though he might have been killed!"

"And what about me?"

"Oh, you... By the way, I had a phone call from the office this morning to say that Mr Swartze will be arriving later today." Tania took the top off a boiled egg.

"Oh? He's coming back sooner than expected isn't he? Does

162

this mean we'll have to look for a fourth for Rhuda Stack? Your friend Emile *is* going to be disappointed."

"That's all taken care of. I couldn't possibly think of disappointing Emile, and you obviously need someone to keep an eye on you, so Jim Atkinson will pick Mr Swartze up and I'll see him when we get back."

"Well I only hope he doesn't get that nose of his tangled up in the works," Dempster said ungraciously.

They parked the Mini and the Ferrari at the end of the rough narrow road where it ran out onto peatbog.

"The tide should be right for crossing the channel," Paul Wilson said, picking up his large rucksack. "But it's seldom low enough to cross without a dip, even in the spring tides. I hope we don't have to swim."

"We've had a gutful of swimming just now," observed Cliff.

"But you swim, don't you, Emile?" Tania smiled. "You even go out for an evening dip."

"I wouldn't dare offer in such talented company," the Sicilian answered smoothly. "But are we all ready to set off?"

"Suppose so, only I can't understand where my climbing harness went to." Paul looked annoyed and puzzled.

"Lost it?"

"I keep it with my other clobber in the storeroom at the hotel, but it wasn't there when I went to collect my gear."

"You can borrow mine," Casini offered. "I can pass it up on the rope to you for the abseils at least."

"That would be great. Thanks, Emile. It'll save a few rope burns round my posterior coming down."

"That system was patented by a eunuch," Cliff grinned.

They walked for some time across the moor, then suddenly the peat hag fell away and there was a narrow ribbon of closely cropped grass; then a high cliff which tumbled sheer to the sea. The Stack reared up before them, like a solitary tooth, filed sharply from the gums of the shoreline, washed by the green saliva of the Atlantic.

"We can't climb that!" Tania gasped, her mouth wide open in apprehension.

"Oh, yes we can," corrected Wilson, cheerfully. "But if I'm to do my part as host, it does look as though I'm going to have to take a swim first. I'll put a double rope across the channel to a peg that's already fixed at the base of the Stack."

"Sort of double roping on a horizontal plane?" Tania asked.

"That's right. It'll give a two way dry passage for you people, at least. We can haul the end through the stack peg when it's time to go home."

"You make it *sound* easy, Paul," Tania observed with misgivings.

Dempster studied the stack in silence, picking out the line with his eye. The route followed the landward side. It didn't look easy to him either and he fervently hoped he'd done enough climbing recently to lead it.

They didn't pause long, but made their way down the cliff. Out to sea orange floats were bobbing about, marking lobster creels. The way down to the shore was broken, but not difficult. Dempster followed Tania and noticed with approval that she moved well on steep ground.

Wilson stripped quickly, revealing a scrawny frame and swimming trunks. But he looked tough enough. Some of the toughest men Cliff had met looked like walking skeletons.

"Where do you want the rope anchored?" Casini asked.

"On that rock face above you." Wilson pointed behind them. "Can you tension it from there?"

"I'll do it," volunteered Dempster. He picked up Wilson's rope as he spoke, and prepared to pay it out as soon as the climber was ready to swim.

"Ugh!" The exclamation accompanied the sticking of a gnarled foot into the water. Old scars were prominent on his legs. Wilson lowered himself gingerly into the channel and a few minutes later, had reached the other side safely. There was a slight swell running. Dripping, he mantel-shelved onto the rock plinth which extended from the base of the Stack, and moved quickly along the flat apron to the bottom of the pinnacle. Gazing upwards, he found what he was looking for — a large ring peg which had been hammered into a crack by a previous party. He removed the doubled rope, and the end of an extra

164

line he had carried over with him, from his waist and clipped it to the peg.

Meanwhile, Cliff had taken the other end of the doubled rope and climbed up to the rock anchor on the shore side. Gradually he pulled it tighter, until it lay horizontally above the water.

"Hey, easy on," shouted Wilson, alarmed. "You'll pull the bloody peg out!" Dempster tied the rope off securely; then returned to the others.

"I'll go across first," decided Casini. "And I'll trail Paul's sack behind me. He can give me a bit of help from the haul line."

"Fine. Take another rope behind you, it'll help Tania over."

"A good idea," Casini smiled at Tania. "I hope you will enjoy this, Tania. There's nothing to worry about."

She gave him an apprehensive grimace, and watched as Casini swung from the suspension rope from his karabiner. As he did so his right stocking worked down revealing a tanned calf.

"That's a nasty gash!" Tania exclaimed. "How did you do that?"

"One of those steel fence posts sticking out of the heather, up by the ninety-pound pool on the Coen, I'm afraid."

"We all seem to have our injuries," she commiserated.

There was little stretch on the rope and Casini moved across smoothly, hand over hand. Dempster turned to Tania and asked quietly, "What night was Emile swimming?"

She looked at him in surprise, then her brows puckered in concentration.

"Let me see. About four nights ago. That's right, it was the evening after our launch sank and I remember thinking some people actually went swimming for pleasure. It was quite late, actually. You'd gone off somewhere with Alasdair. I was, er, wondering when you were going to come back."

"Yes," Cliff said slowly. "It's beginning to fit."

Further conversation was prevented by activity on the other side of the channel. Casini was sorting out climbing gear, and Wilson was rubbing himself down vigorously with a towel which he had produced from his pack. He put on his clothes and pulled a light bri-nylon anorak over his tartan shirt.

"Just relax now," Cliff instructed Tania. "Emile will pull you over. You're quite safe, hanging from that rope. It's a climber's version of a breeches buoy. I'll feed the yellow rope out from this side."

Tania glanced down at him as she hung there, holding the red rope below the karabiner.

"I trust you, Cliff. You know that, don't you?"

"At a time like this, you should put your trust in the ropes," he answered tersely. "They have a combined tensile strength of 12,000 lbs."

"Sometimes I don't think you're quite human," she retorted, thoroughly exasperated, and feeling like stamping her foot — if only there had been ground, not air, beneath it at that moment.

"You may be surprised, one of these days…"

"Ready?" shouted Casini impatiently.

"Okay," Cliff yelled in response. Tania moved slowly across the water, in a series of jerks and pauses.

"I'll look forward to that next surprise, Cliff," was her parting shot as she departed.

Wilson led from the plinth — up cracks in the ocean-washed sandstone. It was tricky, but he moved with easy confidence. He was wearing lightweight climbing boots with cleated rubber soles. Two white ropes hung from his waist; they were being payed out by Casini. The paraphernalia of modern climbing gear also hung from his waist, like keys on the belt of a medieval gaoler. There were assorted aluminium wedges on short wire loops, for insertion into cracks so that karabiner clips could be attached to them; there were pegs too — pegs with eyelets at one end, of high quality chrome molybdenum steel, and he carried a snubnosed hammer in his back pocket; its handle protruded like a policeman's baton.

"How much rope left, Emile?" Wilson shouted down, looking between his legs.

"About seven metres."

"Okay. I'll belay at this ledge." He secured the rope. "Climb when you're ready." Paul's disembodied voice floated down from aloft.

"Right… Coming." The ropes went taut and Casini moved

easily upwards. A couple of minutes later, Dempster followed, moving powerfully, every movement under precise control, no flap, no scrabbling. He made it look ridiculously easy, thought Tania.

The first pitch was an angled tapering crack, slightly overhung. There just didn't seem to be anything to hold on to. When it was her turn to climb, she felt the butterflies in her stomach. Her clenched hands were jammed in the crack, just as Cliff had instructed her, and she could feel the skin breaking under the strain. She gasped for breath, terrified, yet at the same time enjoying it. She scrabbled and fought, an occasional sob escaping her lips. The tight rope was comforting, but, though she knew she couldn't fall, there was the ever-present fear of losing contact with the rock.

The front pair were leading through — the first leading one pitch, then the other would climb past until he had run out the rope again, pausing occasionally to thread the rope through a clip which was attached to an inserted peg or chock. Dempster was climbing well; he could feel it. He knew Tania was having a struggle. She was bloody game though. He had to admit that. This route was no pensioner's constitutional: it required brute arm strength, as well as climbing finesse. He had climbed up a vertical section without using a runner. The others hadn't used one either, unless the last man up had taken it out.

When he was fifty feet above Tania, on delicate incuts which tested the fingers, he saw, above the lip of a ledge, Casini looking over at him with a superior smile.

The Sicilian had a large rock in his hands and looked Cliff straight in the eye.

"Finding it hard — Mr Dempster?"

21

"IF YOU'RE GOING to throw that rock down, Emile, just chuck it well to one side, would you. I forgot to bring my aspirins." Cliff's mind was racing. Casini had chosen a great moment for the showdown. The rock hurtled past him and Tania and exploded far below on the stack plinth.

"That's better," Casini called down. "It makes things much tidier. So many people have accidents with falling rocks."

"Are you all right?" Tania's anxious voice reached him.

"Yes fine," he replied as he moved again. "Emile was just getting in some target practice."

Casini moved on up as Dempster clambered onto the ledge. They had no further conversation.

When they eventually gained the last pitch, Tania was visibly tiring. Her face was pale and she had difficulty in preventing her hands and legs from trembling — an affliction known to climbers as 'the knock'. The other two had reached the summit as Tania joined Cliff on a minute stance.

"Just look at my hands," she wailed. "My fingers are wearing away. I won't be able to use my typewriter for weeks!"

"What a pity," agreed Cliff, rather amused at her concern. "If you keep on climbing, you'll only be able to do shorthand. I'll move off again," he added, preparing to attempt the final pitch. "Try to keep my rope a bit slacker. It's awkward if it drags on a tricky bit."

"Sorry," she apologised. "There are so many things to learn."

"True," he agreed, moving up on tiny holds, the size of peppermints. "It would have been better to start you on an easier route, but you're doing well." Tania glowed inwardly. She had been terrified, especially on that lower pitch which had been desperate. Had she fallen, she would have swung right out into space. Cliff moved up the final steep rock with enviable ability, looming large against the blue sky. Then he was up.

"Okay," his voice drifted down on the breeze. Quickly she unclipped from the belay piton and started to move up. The climbing was easier; the rock steep with a sheer drop to the plinth below her feet. She could see the rising tide lapping the edge of the stack. A shiver of triumph gripped her; her fingers ached, she felt bruised. It was like having sex for the first time. She came up over the edge: three men, the sea and the sky before her. Emotions crowded in on her — the beauty and the freedom; the summit wasn't much bigger than a pulpit. Casini was sitting cross-legged smoking. Paul Wilson handed round chocolate to the others.

"You did exceptionally well, getting up this climb," Casini complimented her.

"I must say," agreed Paul, "I wouldn't like to have tried it for my first route. You'll be off up Stac an Armin next, Tania."

"I suspect you're teasing," she laughed. "What's Stac an thing?"

"Out there," he pointed westwards, "on Boreray, seventy miles out, all covered in gannets. It's close to St Kilda."

"A high one?"

"About two hundred metres. It's the biggest in British waters. Very impressive. The seas are really something, too. The swell has to be seen to be believed."

"I'll take your word for it, Paul. My main preoccupation at the moment," said Tania truthfully, "is how to get down off the stack I'm on."

Dempster straightened up and gazed out to sea. "No problem," he said. "I'll go down first when we're ready and fix the next abseil for Tania. She can follow me."

"Then I think we should move now." Casini rose unexpectedly, spinning his cigarette butt into the distant water. "I have

169

our two ropes ready here for the first abseil. Tania can join you on the first ledge."

"I told Hugh I'd abseiled before," Tania confessed. "But it was on holiday in Norway. Nothing like this." She gave a mock shudder.

Paul, who had been about to make a plea for a longer pause on the summit, saw Tania's genuine trepidation under the bravado, and decided against prolonging the suspense for her. "You'll be quite safe with a top rope," he said. "The anchors are excellent and the rope's new."

Cliff fed Wilson's two white ropes, 150-footers — over the edge and worked a double sling round his thighs in a figure of eight, as a makeshift harness, then he double-checked the summit rock belay before easing himself over the edge like a huge spider and promptly disappearing. When she had mustered the nerve to peer over, Tania saw him arrive on a platform the size of a newspaper.

Casini took it upon himself to show Tania how to fix her sling for abseiling. She had to keep herself from flinching as his hands roved caressingly over her body while he clipped the karabiner through her waist tape. He took the two white ropes and threaded them through the clip.

"Now take the ropes over your left shoulder and down the back. That's the important thing to remember." He pressed her hand with the ropes into her left thigh and held it there. "Now, see, your left hand holds the rope above you while you descend."

"You have a convincing way of explaining things, Emile," she forced a smile.

"Lean well back," contributed Paul, taking a belay position on the summit block for her safety rope. "If you don't, you'll just slide down the face and have even more bruises."

Tania smiled weakly and moved slowly over the edge in trepidation. Instinctively, her left hand gripped the rope tightly.

Dempster looked up and called, "Lean well back, legs apart." His voice lent her a surge of confidence and she moved rapidly down to join him.

"Wow, that was exhilarating. But quite frightening." She smiled.

"You'll get the know-how, but never be too confident. It can be dangerous." He picked up her safety rope which Wilson had dropped down. "You'll go down on that single rope this time, Tania, and I'll belay you from here with the other one."

"Anything you say," she answered, relieved to be safeguarded by Cliff once again.

"Keep to your left when you get down," he warned. "You might just have to swing out onto the end of the plinth if it's awash." She glanced up to see him peering down.

"Any other pleasant surprises in store?" she commented sarcastically. Next moment she found herself above an overhang and realised it would mean a swing of almost twelve feet to gain the edge of the apron. She had obviously taken the wrong descent line.

"Hugh?" she called in a small voice.

"Yes?"

"I'm on an overhang above the water. I'll have to swing and then let go of the abseil rope. I won't be able to get back up to you."

There was a pause then his voice came again. "All right." He sounded worried. "Sure you can make it? Sorry about this cock-up."

"Yes, I think so," she called back, trying not to spiral round. "I'll go down a bit lower yet. Get me some slack, and I'll start swinging. I'm not very comfortable."

"Right. I'll let the safety rope run out free when I feel you dropping."

"That's comforting," she thought to herself. About twelve feet above the waves, she paused to survey the situation. What would happen if she misjudged and let go of the rope too soon? Or too late, perhaps, so that she landed back in the water? She didn't feel she had enough strength to swim even the few feet to the edge of the apron.

She started to swing, her heart in her mouth. She saw that her hands were bleeding. She called urgently for more slack, and he let it out, hanging now in a loop below her sandshoes. She began

171

to pendulum, almost touching the wall of the Stack below the overhang. Before she realised what she was doing, she had let go at the limit of her outward swing.

"Slack!" she screamed. Dempster let more rope run through his hands, hoping she wouldn't be dashed on the rocks. She felt the end of the abseil rope burning as it ran through her hands. Then there was no abseil rope — just space, and the rope snaking behind her. She landed in a heap on the plinth; at the same moment the safety rope jerked her to a halt and knocked all the air out of her lungs. But she was safe; she was down, with the safety rope threatening to pull her backwards into the water.

"Slack, Cliff, slack." Sickeningly, she realised she had used his proper name; but no-one would have heard it anyway: the others were too high above. Dempster's ledge was out of her sight. The Stack loomed like the stern of a liner over the small lagoon formed between the side of the pinnacle and the plinth. The starting point of their climb was just to her left. She pulled again on the safety rope and it came with her as she sank thankfully forward on the bare, cold rock.

"God!" she breathed. "That was a bit of an epic — I'm glad it doesn't happen every day." Her waist was bruised from the harness and her left hand burned across the palm and fingers. She untied from the safety rope, but kept a hold of the end of it. "Right, I'm down. Okay." Dempster came into sight; her neck felt sore as she craned upwards, watching him.

"Wow," he said ruefully as he spiralled down. "Pity about that — I certainly sent you down on the wrong line! You all right?"

"Fine," she smiled weakly as Dempster pendulumed in and landed beside her with the absurd ease of a long-tailed monkey.

"Sorry — I made a bit of a mess of it."

"Oh," she grinned. "It was definitely worth it, just to hear you apologise. It's made my day!"

They moved back along the plinth to where they could see the others. Casini had almost reached the top ledge. They could see Wilson looking down at him. He vanished out of sight when Casini's rope slackened as he arrived on the stance.

"Pull up the side with the knot, Paul," Casini's voice carried like the cry of a fulmar. "Your harness is attached to it."

"Right." They saw a small bundle travelling up the face like a bright orange insect.

"Paul must be wanting to use the harness."

"Yes..." Cliff's eyes narrowed to slits as he stared upwards. "It makes life a bit more comfortable — for the male of the species."

"He's coming now," she pointed. "I can't think how I did that — it looks positively frightening."

"There are easier places, I must admit," answered Cliff casually. He screwed up his eyes again...

It all seemed to happen in a flash. One moment, Wilson was moving slowly backwards; the next, he hurtled down, emitting an unearthly scream which echoed round the cliff and caused fulmars to veer off in alarm. He spun twice, passed within a few feet of Casini, and fell towards the edge of the rock apron. His head smashed against it with a sickening crunch.

22

THERE WAS AN unnerving silence. Even the waves seemed to pause, until one, more arrogant than the rest, washed over the body and drew it gently backwards into the sea. Dempster lunged forward, but a slightly reddish tinge to the green water was all that remained to commemorate the death of Paul Wilson whose body had been committed to the deep.

"What happened?" It was Casini's alarmed voice from above.

"He fell — " Tania's answer had a hysterical edge to it.

Dempster took hold of the situation. "You'd better come down. There's nothing you can do up there."

"Right. I'll pull the ropes down." He started to haul the ropes from above. Presently he shouted, "I'm coming down." On the final abseil ledge he bundled up the 300-foot of rope which Paul had been using. "I'll throw the ropes down to you, Hugh, and use yours for the last bit."

Ropes and a harness landed on the plinth beside Cliff and Tania with a dull thud. Tania flinched away, huddled in a shocked silence, and Cliff silently got on with the business of coiling up the ropes. Wilson's harness had obviously fallen onto Casini's ledge, and he had sent it down clipped to one of the ropes. Cliff examined it closely, but it was intact. What the hell had happened? Had Wilson been careless? Perhaps he had used the abseil karabiner directly from the crutch strap, instead of from the two special loops designed for the purpose? In that case, the end of the harness waistband, leading through a loop at

174

the end of the crutch strap might have crept through its buckle. He knew that the manufacturers recommended that the tape should be led back through the buckle to prevent this. It seemed unbelievable that someone with Wilson's experience could have made such an elementary mistake.

There had been a lot of strange accidents roping off climbs. He knew of half a dozen personally. This made it seven.

Casini spiralled down to the plinth in a temporary sling harness like Cliff's. He unclipped and started to haul down the ropes, both of which eventually fell into the water. He pulled them onto the plinth in silence before approaching Dempster and Tania.

"How on earth did it happen?" He sounded tense and worried. Cliff threw down the harness in front of him.

"Take a look. Seems he didn't use it properly. Just used a krab directly from the crutch strap."

"Krab?"

"Karabiner — on the webbing that goes between the legs. The waistband can slip through the buckle with a direct load on it, if it isn't done up properly."

"Surely he would know that? It is obvious. He always used a harness like this — he mentioned it himself — only he couldn't find it. That's why I suggested he should share mine. I was going to send it up to him for both the abseils. Personally, I am accustomed to use a chest harness, rather than the waist type — but it was the only one I could buy here." He shook his head and glanced at Tania who roused herself and came towards them, before continuing, "For me, I could understand it happening — I am not used to this harness — but to Paul...?"

Tania seemed shattered. White-lipped with shock, she stared at the red stain on the softer pink of the sandstone, unable to speak.

"It looks deep." Casini gazed thoughtfully into the green depths.

Tania shivered. "Did you see what happened, Emile?"

"No. He seemed to go suddenly, twisting as he fell, as if he was starting to turn when the harness gave way."

"Yes, that would happen," Cliff speculated. "His left arm would be whipped up and he'd turn..."

"That must be what occurred," Casini interrupted, watching the girl with the appearance of concern. "But it is not a good place to linger, here. If you will take Tania back to the hotel, I'll go first and go down to the lighthouse and phone the police and the coastguard."

"I don't think there's any hurry for Paul's sake," replied Dempster dryly. "I doubt if they'll ever recover the body. If it's caught in an undertow, even with the weight of his climbing equipment it would travel right up the coast. It could land up in the Pentland Firth, or even beyond. But I suppose we must go through the legal motions."

"I will telephone anyway." Casini spoke decisively and almost impatiently, as he swung away across the doubled rope on his sling harness. By the time Tania and Cliff reached the mainland, Casini had disappeared over the top of the cliff at a surprising speed.

As he coiled up Tania's safety rope they both heard the staccato beat of an engine.

"That's a boat," said Tania, surprised. Dempster looked at his watch for the first time. It was 5.28.

"It must be Alasdair. I suggested he come round."

"Are those his creels out there?"

"Yes."

The dory came into sight round the point of outlying rocks. Caren was with Alasdair. Dempster waved and they came straight in. Alasdair handled the boat skilfully, guiding her through the patchwork of reefs, leading to the channel, then kicked the outboard into reverse as he eased the blunt nose in like a tame flounder. He had seen a figure running over the high headland a few minutes before and guessed that something was wrong.

"What happened?" He raised his voice.

"Wilson's been killed in a fall."

"Where's the body?"

Cliff pointed expressively down into the water.

"Not another death." Caren was still pale, but in control of herself.

"Casini's gone on ahead to tell the coastguard." Cliff caught hold of the prow of the boat.

"I wouldn't take money on that." Alasdair spoke deliberately. "Caren has just been telling me that her brother is signing over the Rhuda estate to Anglo-Italian Oil at six o'clock and your friend Casini has half an hour to get to the dotted line."

"What?" Dempster froze.

"Yes," affirmed Caren. "James has had a further substantial offer for it. Mr Elliot, he's our solicitor, arrived at lunch time. They're meeting the oil company's representatives at Kerse Glen Hotel."

Alasdair interrupted. "I've told her that her brother was being blackmailed into selling."

Kneeling down, Tania had a hold of the starboard gunwhale to prevent the dory from being forced against the rocks by the swell.

"Can Caren take your boat back to Rhuda, Alasdair?" Cliff asked urgently.

"Sure. She knows how to cope."

"Right. Tania, quick, into the boat. Go back with Caren. Ring the police and get hold of Detective Inspector Galloway. Tell him to come to Kerse Glen Hotel. Alasdair, you come with me..." Alasdair was already halfway out of the boat, anticipating the command. Dempster let the boat go as Caren put it into reverse and it pulled out into a small arena of water encircled by ugly rocks. Changing to forward gear, she crept out through the narrow gap, then, passing between two of Alasdair's buoys into deeper water, gave the engine the works. The boat rose and started to plane. By this time, the two men were halfway up the cliff, scrambling sometimes on all fours up the loose and broken rubble. When they reached the top their lungs felt as if they would burst; they scarcely paused, however, and broke into a run which would not have disgraced a seasoned harrier.

"Will you drive, Alasdair?" Cliff shouted as they neared the Mini.

"Yip."

"What's the best way to go?"

"Well, he'll take the new Assynt road, as he has a faster car."

177

Alasdair gulped deep lungfuls of air. "We'll take the coast road, though it's no motorway."

"Any chance of getting there before him?"

"Maybe — he's had about fifteen minutes' start, I should say, but there are more tourists on the Assynt road, and it's quite a bit longer."

Skidding to a halt, they wrenched the car doors open. Alasdair jerked the seat forward and muttered something unprintable about physical abnormalities; simultaneously, Cliff turned the ignition key and the car started with a roar.

"Stop at the first stream," he yelled above the engine.

"What for?"

"Water. Mr Smart Guy has opened the radiator cock. I saw the stain on the gravel."

"Good for you — you quick thinking bugger. We'd have boiled to a halt."

"I've got a climbing helmet behind the seat; it'll do for a filler."

"Right." Alasdair threw the car into gear and it slithered onto the track, gravel spurting in all directions. They took off down the dirt road, actually rising in the air over the crest of a hill. The Mini landed with a bang which took it right down to bottom deflection on its variable shock absorbers, and hurtled on, sliding round the road end that led to the lighthouse. Now they were on tarmac, six-foot wide, with a grass ridge down the centre. A culvert loomed ahead and the car skidded to a halt, leaving two tell-tale streaks of rubber on the road behind.

Cliff leapt out and dived down to the water. Alasdair left the motor turning and whipped up the bonnet. He had removed the heater tank cap as Cliff returned with the first helmet-ful of water; then he reached down swiftly to turn off the watercock of the cross flow radiator.

"It'll take four." Beads of sweat glistened on Alasdair's face as he poured the water in with the dexterity of a practised barman. "We used to change the boots and refuel in sixteen seconds at Rheims," he commented, as Cliff dived back into the ditch. "This will take about two minutes."

"Last one?" Dempster came up for the fifth time.

"Yes." The header tank overflowed. The cap was on. The bonnet slammed, and they were back in the car. Cliff barely had time to close his door before the needle had jumped to 5,000 rpm in second gear. As they approached a blind corner at over a hundred miles per hour, Alasdair held the car in third in the close ratio box.

"What's the back lever for, Cliff?" Alasdair's voice, though raised above the din, sounded calm and level, as he leaned back in his seat.

"Front or rear wheel drive; centre's for all four wheels."

Alasdair tried forward only as he came out of the corner.

"Very nice," he commented approvingly. "Very nice." A sheep moved off the road as they rounded onto a short straight and lost a lump of fleece on the front-wheel arch extension. It didn't even bother to look round, inured to the everyday hazards of modern tourism.

The road to Kerse Glen, via the hamlet of Ned, is one of the most sensational in the British Isles. To be taken over it in the Lotus Mini was an experience which Dempster had no inclination to repeat, even with a world-class driver whose reactions were way ahead of his own.

"I raced a four-wheel drive heap in the Daytona a few years ago," Alasdair shouted conversationally. "They take a bit of getting used to..."

"You seem to be doing all right." Cliff sounded approving above the engine's whine, as Alasdair changed down to fourth for a fast right-hander. The car screamed in protest.

"You're chancing your arm a bit, aren't you, asking Charlie Galloway to join the party?" Alasdair said presently. "After all it's not yet been declared illegal to beat Swartze to the draw on a deal."

"He'll come." Dempster sounded confident, but preoccupied. His mind was going over and over the sight of Wilson's falling body. It wasn't just the terror and the nerve-shattering scream. It was something else.

They roared up an extremely steep hill; both of the limited slip differentials were engaged — Dempster felt the thud as they took up the spin. On one side a stone wall marked the margin of a cliff that fell sheer to the sea; on the other, a steep hillside covered in green whin, the thrusting yellow blossom just emerging. The speedometer registered 94 mph. He remembered glancing apprehensively at it just before the car and caravan loomed dead ahead, completely blocking the road.

There wouldn't have been room for a bicycle to pass, let alone the wide track of the Mini. Alasdair changed down, braking hard, and the transmission took the strain of a crash change from fourth to second. The eight-inch discs heated up as if under a blow torch. There was a layby to their left, but no hope of stopping in time. The caravan had almost reached it. Cliff realised they must surely crash head on, and saw the look of frozen horror on the faces of the elderly driver and his passenger.

Alasdair slammed the transmission stick into forward only and, in the same sweeping motion, put the car into first; the engine note rose two octaves. The Mini dipped alarmingly, as if contemplating a nose-dive, whilst rubber from the CR 65 tyres filled gaps in the tarmac. Their speed was a mere 40 mph, as Alasdair coolly pulled the handbrake and the Mini swung round as if it had alighted on a moving turntable. The wheels spun furiously and a smell of burning rubber permeated the interior of the car. They were now travelling backwards in the same direction and Dempster was certain they were still going to hit the car — a rear-on collision seemed inevitable — when their wheels gripped the solid tarmac below the grit and the car catapulted forwards. Cliff felt his head snapping painfully backwards as they hurtled onwards, in the direction from which they had just come. Fifty yards later, Alasdair repeated the manoeuvre and the Mini turned about again in its own length. The revs had dropped by the time they returned to meet the caravan outfit, which had pulled up incredulously, the bonnet of the car slightly past their side of the layby. Alasdair slowed down, eased the Mini under the nose of the Austin, and waltzed round the loose chippings in the layby, to emerge unscathed on the other side with a clear road ahead.

Cliff wasn't often shaken, but he felt a distinct lump in his throat.

"I suppose that's more difficult in your V12, Alasdair?" he enquired casually.

"Not enough room for it here." Alasdair maintained his deadpan expression as, once again, the car leapt into orbit.

At last they drew near the main Kylesku road and Cliff's eye was caught by a yellow streak. "Casini," he exclaimed. "We've made it!"

The big Ferrari sped down the hill leading to the ferry, gripping the road like a lizard on a ceiling. The Mini took the right-angled corner onto the main road with a sickening skid, tyres howling. A car was coming the other way, but, since the road was now two-way, the motorist merely raised two fingers as the Mini swerved past. Casini had a two-hundred-yard lead over them and a mile to go.

He was already on the top of the steps when they reached the hotel. Not pausing to look back, he passed through the open door. Alasdair parked the Mini alongside the Ferrari and they leapt out and ran up the steps. Cliff was aware of the drone of another engine, the note of a gas turbine, but didn't check his pace as he stormed into the hotel.

23

A STARTLED RECEPTIONIST gaped up in astonishment at the sight of two large bruised and grimly determined men storming into the hotel.

"Mr McBride?" demanded the darker one.

Temporarily bereft of speech, she pointed dumbly along the passageway to where a small lounge had a 'Private' notice pinned to the door. Dempster burst unceremoniously into the room and saw before him a startled company. Five men stood by a table on which documents had been spread. Casini was apparently in the process of being introduced to the dignified, dark-suited older man who Cliff guessed to be Elliot, the McBride family solicitor. Two other men in the room were of a similar, but slicker calibre, one very dark and the other tall and pale. The man in the centre of the group was James McBride, who spoke first.

"Mr Spencer?" He looked distinctly annoyed. "What can I do for you?"

"I'm afraid this is a private meeting," Casini stated firmly. "I must ask you to leave, both of you." He eyed Alasdair with disfavour.

"It's a remarkable transformation, isn't it," observed Dempster conversationally, "from the man witnessing the death of his climbing partner to the businessman in conference, all within one hour."

"A climbing accident?" James McBride said, uncomprehendingly.

"Yes, but I think you tola me you didn't know him. It was Paul Wilson."

"Wilson?" James whispered half incredulously.

"Are you all right, James?" The man Dempster had identified as Mr Elliot spoke quietly and anxiously. The other two men were growing restless and one demanded to know who the intruders were, in a strong Trento accent.

Casini supplied the information with relish. "A so-called Mr Spencer, supposedly in the oil business, actually a freelance thug called Dempster, operating with the blessing of Consolidated Oil, and his accomplice, a local man named MacAlasdair." Momentarily any further argument was drowned by the noise of the turbine outside rising to the deafening crescendo which announced the landing of a helicopter.

"I wouldn't sign anything yet, if I were you, Mr McBride." Cliff deliberately ignored Casini's outburst.

Then the door opened again to admit a slightly breathless but still commanding figure, in an immaculate Savile Row suit, shoes gleaming like polished black marble. Swartze had arrived. He was followed by Tania, and Dempster was reassured to see the solid figures of Inspector Charlie Galloway and Trigger MacKay, both he noted in plain clothes, filling the doorway behind her.

Tania's employer dominated any room he entered as a matter of course.

"Allow me to apologise for the intrusion and introduce myself, gentlemen," he said smoothly. "Swartze, President of Consolidated Oil, my secretary, Miss Olsen, and — er — two colleagues, Mr Galloway and Mr MacKay."

"This seems to be more like a public meeting than a private business matter," remarked the taller of the Italian lawyers, evidently irritated. "We have important matters to discuss, gentlemen — may I suggest you leave us...extremely soon?"

Dempster ignored him and explained to Swartze; "I arrived here just in time to stop Mr McBride from signing Rhuda Estate to Anglo-Italian Oil."

"Stop?" exclaimed the swarthy Italian. "This transaction is perfectly legal — Mr McBride has agreed to sell the estate freehold to our company."

183

"Have you signed anything yet?" Cliff swung round to McBride.

"No, not yet," James replied uncertainly. "But I see no reason — other than this rather rude interruption — to delay me." He had digested the fact of Wilson's death with a guilty relief, after the initial shock. Now he could scarcely believe his good fortune. He sat down at the table and uncapped his fountain pen.

"If you people would remove yourselves, we can get on with our legitimate business," Casini added aggressively.

"Legitimate?" Dempster echoed derisively. There was a lengthy pause.

"Are you suggesting that the business we have in hand which, as has been pointed out, is entirely a private concern, is not legal?" Elliot spoke with the deliberation and dignity of age and long experience.

Dempster turned quietly to the older man. "I think you will wish to advise your client differently, sir, when you hear what I have to say," he said simply. Then he faced James. "Mr McBride, I have evidence to prove that your father was murdered."

The atmosphere in the room was electric. James McBride lurched to his feet, but Dempster continued. "I have good reason to think that John Pollock was murdered by the same man. And I have just left Rhuda sea stack — as has Emile Casini — where Paul Wilson fell to his death a short time ago. A clever way of disposing of Wilson, Emile."

The Italian lawyers were now also on their feet.

"But this is fantastic," stammered James. "Father? He fell into the salmon pool."

"He was pulled into the salmon pool," Cliff corrected.

"But that's not possible. He was fishing. He would have seen anyone in the water. So would my sister and Johnny Bhan..."

While James was shocked into incoherence and appealing to Mr Elliot, who was watching proceedings with increasing concern, Dempster turned and whispered urgently to Alasdair who slipped out of the room.

"He was pulled in," Dempster continued, "by a diver using re-breathing apparatus. With such equipment there are no air

184

bubbles on the surface; a man in a black diving suit would be invisible in the dark salmon pool. He was pulled in by his ankles."

The silence was ominous. James looked at Casini as if he had come from another planet. Then his face contorted with rage and he leapt at the Sicilian. Charlie Galloway stepped between them and caught James by the arms, folding them to his sides. His hands trembled uncontrollably as Charlie sat him down at the table, and he stared at Casini, blind hatred in his eyes. No-one else in the room moved. Casini said nothing for a moment but slowly drew on his cigarette. He gazed impassively round before speaking.

"I presume that you are able to substantiate these wild accusations to these witnesses, Dempster?"

"Of course. Too bad your plan to blow Miss Olsen and me to bits — or at least ensure we both received a dose of anthrax — came to nothing. You tried hard." He bowed grimly. "And that 'accident' at the oil platform had your inimitable stamp, Emile. The thuggery of last night let down the artistic style a bit — "

Alasdair and Trigger came back into the room at that moment and Alasdair gave his friend a brief confirming nod.

"Evidence, Mr Dempster?" Casini's voice held a touch of impatience. "You make such rash statements."

"I think we may have that evidence, Emile." Dempster spoke slowly. "I found your time switch on part of the wreckage of the *Celtic Pioneer's* launch. Neatly done — connected to an ignition fuse, no doubt. The propane gas leaking just enough to ensure that in two hours the correct explosive mixture was ready for firing, precisely when we were off Gruinard Island. Did John Stewart work out the tides for you?" Casini was silent. Swartze was gazing at him intently. Dempster took a deep breath and continued, now addressing the room at large.

"John Pollock was one of this country's leading experts in underwater warfare. He happened to recognise the Spaniard at the Point House, which incidentally is owned by Anglo-Italian Oil. He also saw someone diving at the mouth of the River Bhan. The diver was wearing re-breathing apparatus which, in itself, is rather unusual. As a matter of fact, its primary function is military because it doesn't produce any tell-tale bubbles. What John Pollock saw, gentlemen, was a rehearsal of the murder of the Laird of Rhuda. Access from the river mouth up to the sea pool where the Laird was drowned had to be reccied."

Casini drew on a fresh cigarette and cast a covert glance round the company through its smoke. Old Mr Elliot sat down on a chair, his dignified face plainly registering concern and shock.

"These are very serious accusations, Mr Dempster. I have no idea whát your profession is, but I feel that the police should be informed."

"We have been, sir." Charlie Galloway's deep voice rang out clearly. "I'm Detective Inspector Galloway."

"I thought I recognised your face, Inspector, but I couldn't place you." The solicitor put on his glasses and surveyed the policeman with mild reproach.

"I think you should continue, Mr Dempster," suggested Charlie Galloway. "I'll fill in any other details later."

"Thanks, Inspector."

"And meanwhile, why don't we go off somewhere and get on with our business, James?" Casini produced an attempt at the old charm. "Sign the transfer and then let's have a drink to celebrate? We can leave Mr Dempster to tell his fairy stories to the Inspector and Mr Swartze. After all, he is being paid to think up fantasies."

"I won't sign any paper with which you're involved," answered James categorically.

"That sounds like a wise decision." Mr Elliot stood up again. "I suggest, gentlemen, that this business be postponed."

"I agree," echoed James. "I want to hear everything Mr Dempster has to tell us. You were saying, about this John Pollock?"

"John Pollock went out to the Point House one night. He obviously saw and heard too much. Possibly he saw that Casini was testing sophisticated re-breathing apparatus. During the ensuing struggle, when his air hose was severed, his hand was cut off by the screw of the Point House outboard. But a mistake was made which roused the suspicions of Alasdair MacAlasdair, here, who had been lobster fishing with him."

Between them, Cliff and Alasdair outlined the circumstances of the discovery of the severed hand and the discrepancy of the tides. The atmosphere was very tense and the clang of the steel ramp of the Kylescu ferry carried like a warning gunshot into the quiet room.

"This is all very industrious, Mr Dempster," Casini said eventually, flicking some cigarette ash onto the carpet. "But I really do not understand why you feel obliged to tell *us* all these ingenious theories of yours."

Dempster smiled. "Do you not? Then let me explain further. There is an even more interesting bit of evidence. John Pollock didn't drown without a struggle. He was pulled down, no doubt, by another diver." His fists clenched involuntarily as he looked at Casini. "But when we found his hand there was a small fragment of wool caught in a broken fingernail." Cliff paused and shot a look at Charlie Galloway. "I had it analysed in a London laboratory. It happens to be a very rare wool, as far as this country is concerned, from a primitive Merino sheep and the dye is made from blaeberries. It's a type of wool, in fact, only found in Spain and used by peasants in the Pyrenees. It also happens to match exactly the wool from Bernadino's pullover."

"Aye," Charlie Galloway shifted from one foot to the other almost apologetically, "it may sound a trifle unlikely, but I can confirm that I have had Mr Dempster's private analysis substantiated by Scotland Yard today. Er, would you like to go on with your account of events, Mr Dempster?"

"Then perhaps we could jump a bit to the night of Hector McBride's death. This is how I see what happened: Emile Casini and Bernadino took the launch from the Point House up the coast in darkness to the Bhan, towing the inflatable. The echo sounding taken that night on the launch shows precisely the course taken to the river mouth and corresponds with the Admiralty chart. They would have rowed the rubber boat up to the edge of Bhan Bay. Then Casini swam up the river. The Laird had been fishing every night for ten days at the same spot. Everybody knew he was after the big salmon in the sea pool

187

and it would be no problem for Casini to check his recent movements, down to the very spot he would be standing on."

He turned to the Sicilian who sat impassively, as if dissociating himself from his surroundings.

"You grabbed Hector McBride by his ankles, and pulled him in. He was a strong man and you must have had some difficulty holding him under. A kilt has plenty of buoyancy. In the struggle you got kicked several times — the Laird's brogues are heavy, one came off — and the gaff fouled you and ripped your dry suit, didn't it?" With a lightning movement, Dempster had pulled down the green stocking on Casini's right leg. The gash, though starting to heal over, was obvious to all. Dempster straightened up again. "The rip in the suit corresponds to that gash, wouldn't you agree, Inspector?"

"I would say so, Mr Dempster," the Inspector confirmed.

"Indeed, Inspector? But there is absolutely no way you can prove such a ridiculous assumption," Casini snapped.

"No?" Dempster continued unhurried. "Then I must tell you about Johnny Bhan, one of the gamekeepers from Rhuda. He's a very interesting man. He makes flies."

The expression was explained to the Italian solicitors who were looking increasingly puzzled.

"Fishing flies," Cliff explained. "It's quite an art: fly making. Johnny Bhan made all the Laird's flies. After the 'accident', he took a look at the Laird's fly book, and could tell me exactly which fly McBride had been using — it was the one he had said he was going to try, a Silver Wilkinson with a No 10 down eye, with Johnny's own special lace twist thread ribbing."

"That's correct," James confirmed in a daze. Dempster continued.

"It was a tube fly with a silk body thread and feathers off a goose and a pheasant; special feathers which he always selects with great care. Without any doubt, this was the fly the Laird used on his last night, and he always fished with a 15 lb tapered cast. One of the broken off triple hooks was found embedded in Casini's dry suit. The rest of the fly was caught up on the rollocks on the side of the inflatable. It must have been dislodged from your suit when you climbed back into the boat,

188

Emile. It was your bad luck that Alasdair and I were outside the boathouse when the murder party returned to the Point House, wasn't it? I guess you recognised me before I tumbled to you by that tongue clicking habit you have. Bernadino was unmistakable, of course, even in the dark. And Tania saw you as well when you returned to the hotel — with damp hair."

Dempster looked round the room, smiled briefly at Tania and registered the strategic positions of Alasdair and Trigger MacKay near the door, before leaning back against the large oak table to continue.

"The last act was set at Rhuda Stack today. With the Laird out of the way, his son was willing to sell to Anglo-Italian. So Paul Wilson, who had been applying" — he glanced contemptuously at James — "certain pressures was now superfluous to his requirements. Perhaps he had begun to be greedy? But it was much tidier to rub him out, wasn't it, Emile?"

The Sicilian threw him a look of hatred but made no reply.

"I see you have that rucksack, Constable MacKay?"

Trigger looked at the Inspector who gave a curt nod.

"Aye, I have it," Trigger affirmed in the measured tones befitting one who is well aware of the importance of the piece of evidence he is about to produce and justifiably proud of the deductions he has made from it. Trigger's intelligence did not only operate in the field of firearms. The constable continued, "And I have found the contents rather strange." He drew out a tangle of climbing gear, separated a climbing harness from this and held it up. "Someone appears to have used an acid on this waist tape. I have seen a similar effect when hydrochloric acid was spilt on an old car safety strap by mistake." He handed the harness to Dempster, who examined it briefly.

"Yes, Emile," Cliff resumed the thread. "You lent him your harness, didn't you? Or rather, you gave him a harness which you had doctored, after stealing his from the hotel storeroom. You found out he used a harness and didn't like roping down without one, and last night you put acid on the rear of the harness, where no-one would think of looking, where the two buttock straps join the waistband." He passed the evidence to the Inspector. "When you sent up a harness to Paul, you didn't send up the harness you were wearing. Oh no, you were well hidden on that little ledge. You took it off and bundled it up, as if you were about to tie it onto the rope, but substituted for it the faulty one which was tucked away in your rucksack. Then you shouted for him to haul it up and down he came with a bang. As soon as he put weight on the harness it parted and slid down the rope to your ledge. All you had to do was put it back in your pack and throw your good one down to me with the abseil ropes. It was neatly done."

"You have a very ingenious imagination, Mr Dempster," Casini acknowledged, stubbing his cigarette out in an ashtray. "And," he continued, anger flashing in his eyes, "how did you get into my car, constable? It was locked."

Alasdair answered, mildly. "The offside handle seems to be wrenched off, Mr Casini. I just opened the door as Cliff suggested…"

Casini made a lunge for Alasdair, but the Scotsman's enormous hand shot out and gripped him by the forearm. The Sicilian turned pale, sweat glistening on his forehead, before Alasdair released the pressure.

Charlie Galloway cleared his throat, favoured both Alasdair and Casini with a warning look, which suggested they might be in danger of overstepping the mark, and moved to the centre of the room. He coughed portentously.

"Miss Olsen, gentlemen, until now I have not spoken, because Mr Dempster and his friend Mr MacAlisdair have done a lot of the work on this case and have suffered personally in consequence. Let that speak for itself. Maybe if they had taken us into their confidence sooner, in the matter of the severed hand, we might have made more rapid progress. But then," he smiled bleakly around, "we ourselves did not let it be known that we had suspicions about Mr Pollock's death from the very beginning. That way it made it easier for us to keep a number of people under observation — including you, Mr Casini. We were watching you watching the explosion of the *Celtic Pioneer* launch. The wreckage, by the way, has been washed up south of Strathcon and we discovered wiring and a mercury switch which activates by movement, such as someone stepping aboard.

190

Finally, I should tell you that we have implemented our search warrant for the Point House today. The Spaniard, Bernadino, is in custody. You will be gratified to learn that he did not talk, Mr Casini, but John Stewart had no such compunctions. He had just been making a statement to me when I was called here."

"I do not see any point in wasting more time." The tall pale Italian lawyer spoke with finality. He straightened up, put some papers in his briefcase, while his colleague replaced the top of his pen with a formal nod to the assembled company, they headed for the door. No-one said a word. Casini moved to follow them, but Trigger came forward purposefully.

"You'll be coming with us, Mr Casini," Charlie suggested gently. The two policemen moved to the door, Casini, after a fractional pause, between them, an incongrously jaunty figure in his climbing clothes. He stopped as he came to Tania, made as if to speak, then merely shrugged gracefully and left the room.

As the door closed behind the police and the Sicilian, the atmosphere in the room changed abruptly. The tension had gone. Cliff allowed himself to sink into an easy chair and rubbed his hands over the side of his neck. It was stiffening up as a result of the previous night. He grinned at Alsadair.

"You look a bit motheaten, too."

"It's that bloody doctor," Alasdair winced in memory. "He's got paws like a vibrator. Wouldn't believe I fell through a fish box. D'you know what he said as I was leaving? — 'First time I've seen a fish box made from tongue and groove, MacAlisdair.' "

Across the room Mr Swartze was talking to James McBride and his solicitor, offering his condolences to the younger man and at the same time assessing an advantageous situation. His spectacles flashed in the evening light. After discussions in Dallas about a new refinery for the Thule field he was, he explained, now in a position to offer a substantial increase on Consolidated Oil's original figure.

Tania watched a bemused James and a cautiously attentive Mr Elliot being gradually overcome by the dynamism of the rotund figure which was her boss. It was a spectacle she had witnessed many times in her career, she smiled to herself and turned to join Cliff and Alasdair.

The yellow Ferrari was still parked outside the hotel. Jim Atkinson was leaning almost cheerfully against it. Things, at last, were happening. A police car had just turned and accelerated away. The Ferrari's owner was in the back seat between Trigger and a uniformed policeman. Charlie Galloway in the front passenger seat gave a perfunctory wave.

"What now?" she asked, looking at Alasdair and Cliff in turn.

Cliff opened the door of the Mini for her and smiled.

"Alasdair is going back to make an honest woman of Caren McBride and you are coming on a long vacation with me. Tell Mr Swartze he'll be getting my full report in due course, would you, Jim?"

"And tell him I'm taking some of my long accumulated leave. I hope Emile is off on a really long holiday, too," Tania added.

Cliff grinned. "There'll be less oil under the Minch when he comes out."